I watched her as she paused in the doorway to let her eyes adjust to the watery light admitted by the Wharf Rat's salt-sprayed windows. With hands in pockets and collar turned up against the outdoor chill, she had a young and somewhat vulnerable look. I pegged her at twenty-five, no more. Her hair was dark and curly, cut short against a well-formed head. A straight, rather narrow nose topped a mouth that looked as if it could smile easily. Her eyes were a warm brown, her skin fair. She wasn't terribly tall, maybe five-five or so. But the straight-cut jeans held long dancer's legs. I knew underneath the soft denim would be muscular calves and smooth elongated thighs ending in small solid buttocks that would be the perfect handhold. As she removed her jacket, the high, round little breasts nudged her sweater as if reminding it to touch them gently.

Visit

Bella Books

at

BellaBooks.com


or call our toll-free number

1-800-729-4992

# Caught In The Net

**AN ALEX PERES MYSTERY**

## Jessica Thomas

Bella
BOOKS
2004

**Bella Books, Inc.**
P.O. Box 10543
Tallahassee, FL 32302

Printed in the United States of America on acid-free paper
First Edition

Editor: Karin Kallmaker
Cover designer: Sandy Knowles

**ISBN 1-931513-54-6**

*For Marian Pressler*
*With many thanks for 'giving' me Fargo and his owner,*
*and for being a good friend, near and far.*


*And for my editor, Karin Kallmaker,*
*who guided me through 'the first time'*
*with humor, patience and grace.*

# Chapter 1

We hadn't been looking for trouble that day. We hadn't been looking for anything, actually. But you never know when something is going to show up out of the blue and give you a solid kick in the tail and send you off in another direction. Right direction? Wrong direction? I'm still trying to sort it out. And it will be some time before I do, I can tell you that for certain.

It all happened in Provincetown, that strange and beautiful place where the men are pretty and the women are tough. And I'm one of the women. Not tough looking, actually. At five-eight with hazel eyes and wavy light brownish-red hair, I've been told by my grandmother that I'm beautiful and by my brother that Halloween is my best day.

As I move inexorably toward my mid-thirties, I find that I am less concerned about the one comment and less believing of the other.

Anyway, most of the local straight guys got the message early on in my life not to mess with me. Those that didn't walked a little delicately for a while. Even nowadays I don't worry overmuch about trouble from men, or women either, for that matter. Between my partner and me, there isn't much we can't handle.

My partner, my companion, my playmate and guardian against all things bad: Fargo is my love and my best friend. He's a big ninety-pound black Lab with eager brown eyes and a keen nose and a really glorious deep bell of a bark. He walks ever close and alert by my side and only a fool would hassle me.

But Fargo and I do share a dirty little secret. One fall day, he and I were walking down by the marsh when a nearby duck hunter fired his gun, and I found myself flat on my back in the pine needles as Fargo tried to jump into my arms. Another time, on the beach, he and a chubby little black female Cocker Spaniel had been playing nicely together. They came upon a hamburger wrapper that must have had a tiny piece of food left in it. Fargo assumed it was his— he was bigger, wasn't he?—and reached for it.

The snippy bitch bared every sharp little tooth and charged him. Once again I found myself on my back spitting sand. Once again his leap for safety caused us to leave the field in humiliating defeat. Eventually, I learned to forestall these leaps by grabbing his collar and doing a fast sidestep, but I had to face it. The mighty Fargo was a creampuff.

But he loved me and he made me laugh. He never asked why I was wearing that ratty old sweater, or why I never learned to cook or why I was sometimes late. He looked the protective part and he did his best and we both kept quiet about the other thing. Anyway, I was tough enough for both of us. I was hard because life had been thrown at me hard. And in my business, soft and sweet wouldn't have hacked it anyway.

My business? I'm a private investigator. And how does a rather small resort town like Provincetown support a P.I.? Actually quite nicely, thank you. Don't confuse me with the TV types of investigator. I can't remember when my 9mm Glock was last out of my safe and on my person. Nor does it come immediately to mind the last time a beautiful woman whispered, "Oh, you are so brave. Take me, take me!" ten minutes after meeting me . . . or even twenty.

Still, like any PI, most of my business revolves around the less savory aspects of human nature. Like the tourists, God help us. I've always been fascinated by the change some people undergo the minute they are on vacation and a hundred miles from home, in a place where they are unlikely to run into anyone who knows them. People who, in their hometown would run after a stranger, calling "Stop! You've dropped a quarter back here!" become determined petty thieves on vacation. For instance, although I don't investigate these little nuisances, there is the matter of purloined towels, ashtrays, glasses and salt and pepper sets.

Most middle and lower scale hotels, B&Bs and restaurants long ago gave up monogramming the above items in an effort to avoid theft. It has not worked. An amazing number of tourists walk out with nondescript towels, ashtrays and even bud vases from their rooms. They pocket plain glass salt and pepper sets, all the sugar packets and any cloth napkins found on a restaurant table. Who knows why they do it? No visitor to their homes will know that they lodged at the Bayside Bed and Breakfast or dined at the Savory Seafood Restaurant just from looking at the loot. And the purloiners don't even get a little freebie, since eateries and lodgings factor these thefts into the cost of a meal or room anyway. Go figure.

My work is largely with people whose tendency toward larceny has gone a bit beyond Towels 101. They are usually people who attempt insurance fraud, most often by claiming personal injury. After all, if wearing an Ace bandage and limping a bit for a few days will get you a vacation paid for by an insurance company, why not? I see the same attempts at fraud over and over. Only the names are changed to protect the investigator from dying of boredom from the sameness of the stories.

And their lack of originality is eclipsed only by their greed. The victim-to-be will surreptitiously place a grape, a lemon slice or a pat of butter on the floor of the supermarket, bar or restaurant. Then they carefully step on it, sink to the floor with more or less grace and lie there moaning, "Oh! My back!" or "Ooh, my neck! I'm gonna sue!" It's the same process for guest-house steps or a tricycle fortuitously left on the sidewalk. Or they will walk between the cars of the bumper-to-bumper, turtle-paced traffic of Commercial Street in the summer, fling themselves across a hood and start screaming.

Sometimes the less athletic will arrive at the emergency clinic around 2 a.m., claiming to have gotten food poisoning at a local restaurant, usually an upscale one, figuring they'll get more money. Of course by now the vomiting has usually stopped (if it had ever started), so they are simply given some palliative or other and sent home clutching their proof of having seen a doctor, when they go to threaten the restaurant owner.

How prevalent were these thieves? Enough that no less than four Boston insurance companies kept me on retainer, and several others made sure I was up front in the old Rolodex. They paid me to make a fast, on-the-spot decision regarding potential claims. The obviously or probably legitimate I kicked back to the companies to be handled by their legal departments. The barely legitimate I could usually settle in a hurry and on the spot by waving a few large bills and a release form.

The openly frivolous were the most fun for me. Watching the bastards back down from the million dollars they initially swore they were owed, to a whining, "Look, just forget it, okay? Just forget it," when I threatened them with arrest for attempted fraud was a treat. At this point I usually flashed my private investigator's license, complete with a colorful replica of the Great Seal of Massachusetts. I kept my thumb over the word "private" and it worked like a dream! None of us rests easy around what we presume to be officialdom.

Then there was the occasional arson for me to look into, usually committed by a local resident who figured it might be nice to let the insurance company pay for the new roof. There was one time when

4

a tourist damn near burned down a whole motel rather than pay two days room rent for himself and his family. I got a few divorce cases where one spouse wanted pictorial proof that the other had the nerve to enjoy life somewhere besides home. Once in a while I had to locate a missing heir in order to settle an estate. Fairly frequently, I investigated someone who was on the short list of potential hirees for a sensitive spot with a local company.

The runaways, those were the sad ones. They were usually twelve years old and up, where the parents had some cause to believe—or at least reason to hope—that the kid had headed for Ptown. We rarely found them. Usually they had been detoured— often terminally—long before they got here. Once in awhile we were treated to a tearful yet joyful reunion scene, with fervent assurances on both sides that family relations would improve. It kind of gave you that worthwhile, God's in His Heaven feeling. For about an hour.

Most of this activity took place between April and October. After that, the majority of Provincetown more or less shut down until the spring, when once again the tourists would grace us with their heartily welcome, thoroughly despised presence. October to April was a time when most residents rested, went on vacation, repaired, redecorated—and drank.

I had already done the first four and was trying not to do too much of the fifth (no pun intended) until things picked up again. It was March now, so at least the days were longer and brighter. Still, I was sufficiently bored to be whiling away the lunch hour at my "other office" in the Wharf Rat Bar and happy to have picked up a small "case" that morning.

I had received a call from one Diane Miller, who wanted to see me "right away" on a "vitally important and sensitive personal matter." People who had finally worked up the courage to call a PI always needed them "right away," before—I suppose—they lost their nerve again and canceled.

I had visited the home of Ms. Miller that morning, and found her flopped moodily on a spotty couch, listening to a woman on a TV talk show confessing with obvious relish to a series of sexual exploits that would have put Caligula to shame. Ms. Miller's four-year-old daughter was sketching on the picture window with a chocolate chip cookie, while her two-year old son rattled the bars of his so-called "play pen" cage and screamed.

Has any kid ever actually played in a "play pen"? All the ones I've ever seen seem to be practicing to rattle jailhouse bars, shriek their innocence and demand a lawyer, preferably at the taxpayers' expense. Neither the house nor its occupants looked particularly appetizing, and I wondered briefly if the urgent problem might be to find a housekeeper and/or nursemaid. Finally, the TV was turned off, the daughter wrapped up and sent out to play and the son's screeches assuaged by the remains of his sister's cookie.

Unsurprisingly, Ms. Miller was "certain" that her husband Raymond was ah, seeing another . . . you know, woman and that she wanted some . . . ah, you know, information and . . . ah, pictures that would fix the son-of-a-bitch in case they were ever needed in, you know . . . court.

She had been delighted when I told her I would log her husband's activities during whatever hours she specified and would take pictures of him entering or leaving any buildings at that time, alone or accompanied. Disappointment came when I explained I would not climb trees and peer through windows nor burst through locked boudoir doors to supply her with sexually explicit photos with which to pass the lonely hours. Outrage followed when I quoted my rates, and she almost told me to leave, which wouldn't have particularly upset me. I didn't much like domestic cases, and I didn't much like what I had seen of the Miller family either.

I shoved the notes from my morning meeting in my pocket and took a belt of my beer, looking around from my back corner table at the Rat. In the summer most visitors seemed pleased by the deter-minedly nautical decor. Lobster pots and fishing nets hung from the ceiling, with starfish, crab and oyster shells hooked in them. The walls held binnacle lights, oars, buoys and ancient life preservers stuffed with cork. The tables boasted clam or scallop shell ashtrays. In one corner stood the engine room telegraph from a long-retired ferry, its indicator frozen on "All Astern Slow," which seemed a proper designation for the Wharf Rat. Those of us who lived in Provincetown year-round had long since ceased to notice the decor, unless its generous coating of dust became caught up in a sneeze-provoking errant breeze.

As I checked out the other occupants of the bar I realized the late winter doldrums were still upon us. Customers were few. A couple of businessmen eating lunch. A single gal at the bar. I knew her. She would still be there at closing. Several fishermen gathered around a table toward the front. Harmon, more loose-tongued than his friends, argued loudly, "If the feds are going to make fish illegal with these damn quotas, you know some folks'll find something that's worth more money."

His buddies grunted in surly agreement and the conversation was off and away on the ever-popular talk of drug runners. Everybody "knew" that "millions of dollars were made everyday" bringing drugs onto the Cape in certain fishing boats. Some drugs came in through New Bedford, some through Provincetown. They were picked up at sea from other fishing boats or various cargo ships and brought ashore, where they were variously disseminated—perhaps wind-borne—throughout New England.

I listened with half a mind. Maybe everybody "knew," but nobody seemed able to "prove," so what was all the posturing about? When I heard one man say confidentially that he had it on high authority that the drugs were being landed on Truro Beach from a Pakistani submarine, I knew it was time to get some fresh air.

When I got in the car, Fargo greeted me with a sorrowing look that told me I'd been gone too long to suit him. "Mea culpa, Fargo, how about a run on the beach?" He lapped at my face and wagged his tail in a circle that I took to mean yes, and we drove out to Race Point. It's usually deserted this time of year, but there was one other vehicle in the lot, a large van with Jersey plates and a noisy family of four eating sandwiches. No matter what the season, the tourists are never *quite* gone these days—the only cash crop left that is both legal and without quota.

The storm from the night before had left as swiftly as it had come, and the empty beach was littered with the detritus the sea doesn't want and flings back at us from time to time: fishermen's boots, heavy gloves, tangled lines, plastic boxes, broken lobster pots, cans and bottles mixed among the more natural and less objectionable litter of logs, seaweed and shells. I wished I'd brought my camera. Post-storm debris often provided dramatic or even humorous combinations of items for great photos. And I take a lot of photos. It's not just a hobby with me, but also a sort of secondary job that's rewarding, both emotionally and financially. There's a good and growing market, and I enjoy tapping into it. The camera, however, was safely—and uselessly—at home.

But the sky was that bright clear blue it only gets to be after a storm, and the sea was a calm blue-green with delicate little wavelets lisping almost apologetically along the shoreline. It didn't get much better.

Fargo had gone ahead of me, running off some of his incredible energy. He plunged in and out of the shallow water as if it were August, stopping now and then to dig frantically at some small burrowing critter which he never caught and probably didn't want to. Then he went up on the dry sand to check out something that had been cast ashore.

He looked at it sideways and then barked. He pawed at it, backed off and wagged his tail and barked again. I called him but he didn't come. Now that was rare and I started toward him. I really hoped he hadn't found some small animal or bird alive and wounded by the storm. I wasn't in the mood to deal with it.

I caught up with him, collared him and pulled him away. It was only a man's sneaker. What the hell did he find so fascinating about that? Then I realized I really wasn't going to be in the mood to deal with this.

Inside the sneaker was a foot.

# Chapter 2

Having been unfairly yelled at and yanked around, Fargo sat staring out to sea with a sour look on his face, thinking—no doubt—of the many injustices he suffered in our relationship. I stood beside him, staring out to sea with a sour taste in my mouth, trying not to think about that effing sneaker with the white bone sticking up, sheared off rather neatly right above the ankle, and the pale, porcine-looking flesh that surrounded it. Where the bloody hell had it come from?

Oh, it came via the sea, of course. I knew that. But *where* in the sea? From the looks of it, it had to have been cut off by a boat propeller or some other machinery . . . or perhaps a saw. Not that I was any expert, but somehow it did not look as if it had been surgically removed. Anyway, I thought, with only a marginally hysterical giggle, wouldn't the surgeon have removed the shoe before he removed the foot?

If someone had fallen overboard or been injured on a fishing boat or pleasure craft from Provincetown, I would have heard right away—along with all the rest of the town. If the boat were from another Cape town, it would have been on the news, both electronic and word of mouth, long before now. I found it hard to believe it was some illegally dumped hospital garbage gone hideously astray. Didn't they cremate amputated body parts, anyway? And the accident—surgery?—attack?—had to have happened nearby. It hadn't been in the water that long.

I don't like mysteries. They bother me. That's why I try to solve them, although I had never before encountered one that involved a disembodied foot. But for some reason I wanted no part of this one. I had a great desire to collect my dog, go home, pour a stiff drink and watch cartoons, or a preseason baseball game, which was about the same thing.

But there were two reasons I couldn't do that. One, it really was a police matter. Two, I saw the two kids from the van now playing on the beach. Frankly, I am not a great admirer of children as a species—the younger ones smell funny and the older ones look as if they know something you don't—but even I didn't want two young kids stumbling onto this piece of flotsam or jetsam or whatever you called a lost/discarded body part. I spotted a broken lobster pot on the beach and fetched it back, and placed it over the foot, trying not to look too closely at what I was doing. Then I gave Fargo an apologetic pat, told him to come along and headed for my car and cell phone.

As I climbed the hill and made a detour toward the van, the tourist-parents watched me warily from the van's front seat. I didn't really blame them. I was windblown, panting from the climb and probably a little wild-eyed as I walked over to the vehicle. The husband rolled his window down a scant two inches. "Yeah?" he greeted me cordially.

"Sorry to bother you," I said, "But there's something on the beach you'd probably rather your kids didn't see. You might want to

10

call them." The father gave me a sharp look, opened the door and edged out around me, walking off the tarmac down onto the sand, where he began yelling and waving at his offspring.

The mother seemed to thaw a bit with this domestic conversation and leaned across the driver's seat toward me. "What is it you saw down there?" she asked. "Some poor dead dog or cat, I suppose?"

"No. It's a man's foot."

She shot out the passenger door and ran to her husband, speaking wildly, yanking his arm and pointing first toward me, then the beach, then back to me. The man ran down the beach and shooed his kids up the dune and into the van. They drove off in a roar, the man having trouble with the clutch. I looked after their departure enviously and walked to my car.

I sat behind the wheel and took a pack of cigarettes off the dashboard and lit one of the five I allow myself each day. I allow myself five. The other eight or ten I smoke are not allowed. Look, I try to watch my weight, I try to watch the booze, I try to remember my vitamins, I love my mother. Get off my case. I got the cell phone out of the compartment and phoned 911.

"Provincetown Police Department, Officer Mitchell speaking."

"Hi, Mitch, It's Alex." My name is Alexandra, but don't call me that unless you are my mother or my Aunt Mae. "Is Sonny there?"

In a moment I heard, "Sergeant Peres, may I help you?"

"Hi, Sonny. It's Alex." I told him my sad tale.

His reaction was much like mine. "Shit." He sighed heavily. "I suppose you're absolutely sure. I mean, it couldn't be some kind of toy or one of those things from a joke shop or something?"

"Sonny, I know a foot when I see one, even one that's disconnected."

"Yeah, sorry. It's just that I hate these things. We'll have a hundred pounds of paperwork and never find the . . . owner. Well, stay put. We'll be right out."

Provincetown Detective Sgt. Edward J. Peres—Sonny—is my older and only brother. I guess you'd say we are pretty close. My brother, my mother and I had always been close. Life with father rather guaranteed it.

Musing on my father's legacy was perhaps more pleasant than musing on an amputated foot, however marginally. But once begun, of course, my stroll down memory lane would not be denied.

Daddy Dearest had been an assistant manager at the A&P. He worked hard, put in long and weird hours and got paid never quite enough. In his few off hours he drank. When he *was* home, he was either insincerely jolly, or sorry for himself or cuttingly sarcastic or asleep. Mother at least was consistent. She tried to please everyone and so, of course, pleased no one—least of all herself, I imagine. But she never quite lost her sense of humor, and she loved us and we loved her back.

When Sonny was fourteen and I was twelve, the tip of the Cape caught the tip of a Class 4 hurricane. There was a savage and unrelenting wind, sheeting rain and no electric power by late afternoon. They barricaded and closed the store early. Dad fought his way home through crowded, flooded streets to a cold house and cold sandwiches in the dark, with no TV, only a candle to see by and the wind howling voraciously through cracks we hadn't known the house had. The only sensible thing to him seemed to be drinking himself to sleep.

The next morning we woke from what little sleep we had managed to a strong wind and merely heavy rain but still no power. Dad began his day with no hot water for a shower, no hot coffee and no hot breakfast to soothe what must have been the mother of all hangovers. To complete his already miserable day, two power lines threaded their way across our driveway, blocking his exit.

He called the power company and got little joy there. A recorded message told him the power company was doing its best and to be patient, and then compounded his irritation by adding a stern warning not to go near any downed wires even if they looked safe. He muttered and paced for about a half hour, then threw on his raincoat and said, "The hell with it, I've watched those wires for twenty solid minutes and they haven't sparked once. They can't be live. And I've got to get to work. God knows what shape things are in down there."

He walked down the drive and, standing in a puddle, with rain running down his face, he picked up one of the lines. The doctor estimated that he had only one or two seconds to realize his error. His wife and two children had a number of years to think upon his stupidity.

The money from a company insurance policy (Dad's only provision in that line) seemed to diminish daily. Mom brushed up on some old secretarial skills and found a job at the Catholic church-office, which also provided some very welcome benefits. Sonny and I did what we could after school and during the summers. And somehow we made it.

Of course, many things changed. I did not become a lawyer. I did manage to put in two years at the community college in Hyannis, pass my exam for private investigator's license and start to build a business. It wasn't easy. I was young and female and the town was small. Many people knew me and were uneasy about trusting their confidential business to someone they saw regularly in the market or with whom they'd gone to high school. But I stuck it out and slowly it pulled together.

In some ways I knew it would be a lot simpler to practice my trade in a large city, but I didn't want a large city. I wanted Provincetown, with its rickety old buildings along Commercial Street and its side streets of crowded dwellings. I wanted the smell of the sea and the expanse of the dunes and the stunted little scrub trees in the pine woods. I wanted the carnival hysteria of the summer and the clear cold solitary beauty of the winter. I wanted the continuum of the old people I had known all my life and the kids who would know me all of theirs. And so, I stayed. And I am not sorry.

Sonny did not become an airline pilot. But he came back, too, after a couple of years in the army. He sort of drifted into the police department, but he found a home. Sonny became a good cop. He didn't take any nonsense off of anybody, but he wasn't a bully, either. He took a bunch of correspondence courses in criminal law and police procedure and went over to Boston a couple of times a year for seminars in various subjects. He would be chief of police one day, and the town would be the better for it.

I had to admit he would make a good looking one. He was fairly tall, with a good build and cute buns. Unlike me (who looked much like our mother) he took after our Portuguese father in coloring, with dark wavy hair and skin that always looked tanned. A badly set nose, broken by an outraged young lady when he was fifteen, just kept him from being pretty.

Nowadays it was about fifty-fifty whether the girls or the boys found him more attractive. But there was no doubt in Sonny's mind: he liked the girls. So well that he had two ex-wives and three kids scattered along Route 6. Right now, he lived at Mom's. It was about the best place he could afford under the circumstances, especially since it included home-cooked meals at all hours and a crisp uniform always hanging in the closet.

But I shouldn't be snide about Sonny's less than perfect love life. I had a few exes of my own strewn about, although at least I wasn't into child support. I did not live with Mom, had gotten my own place years ago and finally bought it. Living with her would not have worked for me. While she completely and warmly supported my being gay, I had the feeling she preferred not being reminded of its more intimate details on a daily basis. And while neither my brother nor I would dream of sneaking a girlfriend into a bedroom at Mom's house, if Sonny stayed out all night it was simply ignored. If I did, it would result in a lecture. Men had needs. Women had reputations.

And another of Sonny's needs was to be a bit of a cowboy. Here he came now, leading a convoy of two police cars up the hill, lights flashing, sirens whooping. They skidded to a stop in front of me. Sonny came back to my car, walking daintily to keep the sand from scuffing his shiny low cut boots.

"Gee, Sonny, did you need to bring an army? You think we're being invaded by the Feet People?"

"Never can tell, the rest of him might be lurking in the bushes."

"If he is, I don't think you have to worry too much about his catching you. He ain't gonna run too fast."

"No." He reached across the steering wheel to pet the grinning Fargo. "Yeah, boy, you had to go and find it didn't you, boy? Well, where is it?"

I pointed down the beach. "Under that lobster pot. I put the pot over it. There were little kids playing on the beach, and I was afraid they might spot it. They left with their parents. A blue Ford van with Jersey plates. I don't think they had anything to do with it. They looked typical tourist to me, scared to death and took off like a flock of sparrows at a cat convention. But here's their license number anyway."

He stuck the scrap of paper in his shirt pocket and turned to his three minions, telling them to take various photographs, collect the foot, check the area for footprints and look around for any other body parts. (I was glad I hadn't thought of that possibility.) In a short while the men returned, their search obviously fruitless except for the original item, now in a black garbage bag being swung casually by a gum-chewing young cop. It seemed sort of informal to me, but, I told myself, they could hardly be expected to parade around with it on their shoulders like a bunch of pallbearers either.

Sonny gave Fargo a final ear-scratch. "I'll let you know if we find out anything. But I wouldn't hold my breath."

Fargo and I went home. I, at least, was ready to call it a day. I had a long soak in a hot tub and got out thinking of an evening in cozy flannel pajamas watching the Celtics. Then I remembered I had to play Snoopy for Ms. Miller. Damn. Tiredly, I pulled on lined jeans, heavy socks and boots, and a long-sleeved teeshirt. I'd add a sweatshirt and jacket to that when I went out. It would be cold sitting in the car while I waited for Raymond Miller to do whatever it was he did.

I fed Fargo and checked the freezer for some culinary delight for myself. I settled on a macaroni and cheese dinner plus one of those little containers of applesauce. Somehow meat didn't appeal to me tonight.

A short while later, Fargo and I set out for the Miller residence, set neatly in a development off Shank Painter Road. I parked up the hill a bit, where I could watch his driveway, and, just as his wife had predicted, he drove out at seven-thirty. I followed him down near Town Hall to the building that held his office. Shortly after he disappeared inside, lights went on in a second-floor office. Maybe he really did work nights. But no, the lights were just a decoy. He left them on, came out again, and we followed him slowly, rolling quietly along with the car lights off, as he strolled over to the Fisherman's Bar and Grill.

Fargo and I settled down, cuddled together, to see whom he would come out with. There were enough people and cars on the street that I wasn't worried about being spotted by Miller or anyone else.

So I thought about the foot. Male, almost certainly. Large man, probably, but hard to tell without the rest of the body. Anyway, the sneaker had looked big to me. Fresh? I thought so. Medical waste, probably not. There hadn't been any instances around here of illegal dumping for a long time. And I really was ninety percent sure a medically amputated foot would not have been wearing a shoe.

The shoe itself was just like a million other sneakers and had no special marks that I had noticed. No footprints in the area except mine, so it had doubtless washed ashore. No news about boating accidents. I had caught the news on TV and given the paper a swift perusal. If that held true, then all I could think of was some sort of drug scene.

God, could Harmon actually be on to something? Maybe some dealer had met a "mother ship" recently and perhaps tried to pull a fast one by holding back money or making a fuss over poor quality stuff. Maybe they threw him overboard and his foot caught in the propeller. Or maybe they chopped it off with an ax and sent the rest of him back somewhere (Alive? It might pay to check hospitals.) as some sort of lesson to him and his cohorts. Or maybe some neighbor had cut off his foot with the lawn mower and tried to give it a Viking funeral. Or maybe . . .

. . . maybe I was falling asleep. I sat up with a start. God, it was cold! I gave Fargo a small drink poured into a little bowl from a bottle of water I keep in the car. I gave me a small black coffee from a thermos. Not very much in either case. I didn't want either of us to be squatting behind a friendly bush when Ray Miller came out of the bar with Wonder Woman and disappeared into the night without us. That's a very embarrassing way to lose someone you're supposed to be following. Unfortunately, I know.

Ray Miller didn't come out at all till damn near closing time, and when he did, it was with two other bean counter types (male), one of whom I recognized from the bank. How thrilling. They said goodnight to each other and parted on the sidewalk but just to be completely reliable, I snapped a couple of photos. I didn't think any of them were gay, but who ever knows. I followed Ray, first back to his office to turn off the lights, then toward his home. When he turned into his street, I kept going.

I crawled wearily into bed, shivering. Fargo jumped up on the bed and I was glad of his solid warmth. The end of another exciting day of romance and adventure in the fascinating life of Peres, P.I. The TV networks would be contacting me any day now about a series. Perhaps, I thought, as I began to doze, they would call it *Footloose and Fancy Free.*

# Chapter 3

I'd always liked to fool around with photography. No, not the kind I was doing for Diane Miller. That was probably the one part of my job I heartily disliked. What I liked was nature photos of stuff like I'd seen on the beach yesterday—before the foot—or just oddball things that caught my interest . . . like a bird sitting in the rain looking dour or an old shanty with a cat sunning in the window or a fishing boat with a dog asleep on the nets.

I worked mostly black and white, but some color. I had discovered that other people liked my photos, too. And I had learned that if I enlarged them, matted them and put a simple wood frame around them, people would pay what I considered ridiculous sums for them. I sold quite a few prints, numbered of course to make them look more valuable, through art galleries in the spring, summer and autumn.

This morning I was putting twelve prints into frames to take into Wellfleet tomorrow. One gallery there actually did enough business to stay open all winter. I would go down with a dozen photos. Jay would take nine or ten on consignment. I always took an extra two or three because he always needed a couple of throwaways.

It was like a carefully rehearsed act. He'd line them up, look at them carefully, hand me back two or three, purse his lips and say, "Alex, these are good but I just don't quite think these are meant for *us*." What constituted not meant for us I never had figured out. The ones he refused tomorrow, he might well accept in June. Whatever—he set gratifyingly high selling prices on them. He sold at least some year-round and a lot in season, and he was honest.

Through the window of my combination studio/office I saw Sonny pull into the driveway. I waved and motioned him in. In a few moments I heard him fall to the floor in the living room to begin his usual noisy wrestling match with Fargo. I finished the last photo frame to the accompaniment of howls, growls, barks, thumps and laughter. When I got to the kitchen, I poured two coffees for Sonny and me plus fresh water for the third party. When Sonny had seated himself at the kitchen table and had a sip of his coffee, I could contain my curiosity no longer. "Any news on the foot? Did you find out who it belongs to? And how it got to Race Point?"

"Yes. No. Maybe."

"That certainly clarifies matters," I replied sweetly. "Now I understand the whole thing perfectly. What is the confusion?"

"I'm not confused. But I think the State Police may be. They're thinking it was some kind of complicated drug war on land, air and sea. Personally, I think it's simpler than that."

"Oh?"

"Yeah. Here's what we know so far. We sent your foot—"

"Don't call it *my* foot!"

"Okay. Naturally, we sent *the* foot down to the pathology lab at Hyannis. No news from them yet. Hurry is not in their dictionary. But old Doc Marsten took a look at it here first. I asked him to, just to get some sort of feel for what happened. This is not cast in stone, but Marsten is a pretty good old-fashioned doctor. He says a white male, maybe late twenties or early thirties. Probably at least five-feet ten inches, good-sized guy. The foot was in the water less than forty-eight hours, maybe a lot less, and was probably lopped off by a boat propeller. So, yes, there is some news on yo—the foot."

"Thank you. I'm assuming Marsten verified that it wasn't some kind of medical waste. Even he should know that much. Now what about maybe?"

Sonny sipped his coffee and nodded appreciatively. "You make good coffee, Alex. Mom's always tastes like it's been through the grounds three times. Yes, of course Marsten knew it wasn't medical waste, he says no way was that foot surgically amputated."

I sighed. "I was sort of hoping it was. Gross but simple."

"Yeah, I know. Now, as for maybe, I think *maybe* I know what happened. Well, let me back up a little bit first. In the past few months there have been a series of off-Cape armed robberies with the same *modus operandi*." I grinned at Sonny's careful use of Latin, and he looked irritated.

He continued with a scowl. "This male duo picks an area where there are liquor stores, mom-and-pops, filling stations, dry cleaners, etc. All near each other but not connected in a strip mall, so there are fewer people clustered around at any given time who might witness anything, you understand?"

"I'm with you. And they rob these neighboring stores?"

"Yes. Just before closing time, when most people are home eating or watching TV or whatever. And they haven't been caught for at least two other good reasons. One, they've been hitting stores all over the place. One week they're in New Jersey, next week Long Island, then Vermont, the week after that Connecticut, never the same area twice in a row. Second, nobody can seem to get a make on the car. Like—New Jersey witnesses say they may have seen a tan Escort in the area and Long Island says a blue Toyota, if you see what I mean?"

"Maybe the cars are stolen," I contributed.

"That's what I thought," he agreed. "But they aren't turning up *reported* stolen anywhere." He also negated my next idea. "And they aren't rentals. And nobody has come up with a license plate number so far."

"Witnesses, where are they when you need 'em?" I lamented.

"Stone deaf, sight impaired and passed-out drunk. Anyway, the other night, the night of the storm, they hit the Plymouth area. These are not nice people, Alex. In every instance, even though the clerks or store owners don't argue with them, they sometimes belt them in the head with a pistol to knock them out, they tie them up tight and gag them. Really rough."

"Lovely pair," I murmured sourly.

"Right. Some of them have laid that way all night. Hurt, cold, circulation cut off. One or two have been permanently injured. And, finally, Monday night they really did it. They cut a swath through the Plymouth outskirts and at the last store they hit, they shot a poor half-blind old liquor store owner in the head—he's dead. Bastards."

I liked my brother for still being capable of outrage. But I wasn't making any connection between Johnnie and Clyde and my . . . *the* foot.

"Okay." Sonny absently held out his mug and I as absently poured. "Here's where it gets interesting, to me, anyway. Two kids saw the killers come out of the liquor store . . . lucky the boys didn't get killed for being at the wrong place at the wrong time. Anyway, like most witnesses, their stories are all over the lot—but the consensus is, they saw two men. One white, tall and fairly large around thirty to forty years old. The Plymouth detective thinks he may have been closer to thirty. Everybody looks older to teenagers. The other man was a lot younger, slight, maybe Hispanic or even Italian with a wimpy mustache. They took off in a dark Honda or maybe an Acura."

"Large white male, maybe somewhere in his thirties," I repeated. "That fits the foot if old Marsten is not completely senile."

"He's not. He's sharp about stuff like that. Hell, when he studied medicine it wasn't all computers, you had to know things."

"If you say so." I was not a member of the Marsten fan club.

"And now things get really interesting. I just talked to a guy I know on the Plymouth police force. Near the liquor store where the old guy was killed, there is a marina. It's pretty well shut down this time of year, of course, but they have a guard at the gate because there are valuable boats both in and out of the water that are kept there year-round."

Sonny cadged a cigarette. He only smoked mine, I think. "Well, a couple of lovers go down there around midnight for a little whatever, figuring it's deserted. They hear somebody yelling for help. It's the guy in the guard shack. He slipped the gag after he came to from being bopped on the head. He's tied up but not badly hurt, and he later describes essentially the same two men as the teenage boys did."

"Your plot is thickening, bro." I got up for more sugar.

"Turning into regular pea soup, it is. Now hear this, down the street behind a filling station they find a navy blue Acura. Stolen New Jersey plates, but no record of the car itself being stolen, and the VIN number scraped off. The State Police are trying to get a line on that. Now, you wanta bet they find a boat is missing from that yard? You just wanta bet?"

"Wel-l-l . . ." I thought I saw where he was going but didn't understand his growing excitement. "There are a couple of possibilities, Sonny. If we assume the Acura is the killers' car, they could have parked it behind the building and are hiding somewhere in Plymouth. Maybe with friends, or maybe that's where they literally are from, and they just deserted the car and walked home. Or, they could have parked it and been picked up in another car by an accomplice. No prints, I assume."

He shook his head. "Wiped clean, even in the places most people forget. Anyway, if they left the scene, then why take out the marina guard?"

"Because, dear brother, he's like Everest. He was there. He saw—or they thought he saw—something incriminating. Incidentally, were you aware that Mount Everest is moving to the northeast at six centimeters a year?"

"Where the hell did you get that?"

"I read it in a poem."

"Well, that certainly makes it gospel. Fortunately, I guess it will be a while before Vladivostok is threatened, and I can't tell you what a relief *that* is! You know, sometimes I worry about you, Alex." He stared at me for a moment.

I favored him with a sad, resigned smile. "It's my deep intellectual bent. You have trouble identifying, so it frightens you."

"Oh, okay. Now, where the hell were we? Ah, yes. You could be right, but when you see a boatyard, you think of boats, right? Maybe they met up with an accomplice there who had a boat waiting for them, or they could have stashed one there earlier, or maybe they just bopped the guard and took one that was already moored there."

"On a stormy night?"

"A fair size boat would have done all right in that weather if someone knew how to handle it properly. Anyway, the storm was pretty well blown out by midnight. The marina manager was to run a check this morning to see if anything is missing. I haven't heard yet." Obviously Sonny was determined to get a boat into this, and now I thought I knew why.

"But why would they come here?" I asked.

"Because it's the simplest. Straight across the bay and into sheltered waters. Maybe they have a house here. Or friends. They're here, Alex, I just feel it!"

"Okay, Sonny, I'll give you the boat. At least that docs explain the foot," I conceded. "The big guy must somehow have fallen or been pushed overboard and hit the propeller, and the foot washed ashore in the storm. But, Sonny, there is no way in the world he could be here alive. He'd have lost a helluva lot of blood, been in shock, suffering from exposure. Without some fast, extensive medical attention he'd be dead long since." I paused thoughtfully. "Unless old Doc Marsten is the sheltering friend."

"Jesus, Alex, what have you got against Doc Marsten?"

"See this scar?" I held up my hand. "When I was a kid I broke a glass and cut my hand. Mom took me to him. The sonofabitch said

23

he was out of the stuff that freezes your skin, and he just whipped out this enormous needle and sewed it up anyway, told me big girls didn't cry. I think he enjoyed it."

Sonny laughed and I wanted to slap him. "He probably never had any in the first place. He would figure that was some 'modern gimcrack' and that a little pain never killed anybody. But you are right about Mr. Foot. Even if he got to shore, he'd have to get immediate medical attention or die. And we checked, no clinic or doctor from here to Hyannis has treated any wound resembling that. So scratch Mr. Foot. He's dead somewhere, probably at sea. That leaves his young friend. As far as we know he's not hurt. He's here somewhere."

I wanted to get him off this track. All his life Sonny got 'stuck' on things. As a boy he was determined to build a moon rocket and blew off most of the garage roof. Then he was going to be a figure skater and managed to break his ankle and chip his front tooth. He was going to find the perfect woman and might yet die—or be killed—trying.

Now he was stuck on having a murderer in our midst. Well, to the best of my knowledge, Sonny had never been involved in solving a murder. I guess the closest thing to it had been when old Mrs. Cook's husband died and she kept his body in the freezer so she could keep getting his retirement checks. Maybe Sonny felt you weren't truly a cop till you'd solved a murder. He wanted that little guy to be in Provincetown, even if he had to go somewhere and catch him and bring him here.

I asked quietly, "Then where is the boat?"

"I know. That's a problem. But there are plenty of private docks where it wouldn't be noticed. Or, hell, it could be on the bottom off the end of the breakwater. Who would know? I tell you, Alex, you keep an eye out for that young Hispanic kid. Not many strangers come to Provincetown in the winter." He stood and petted Fargo. "I've got to get going. Thanks for the coffee. You'll catch my killer for me, won't you, boy?" Fargo wagged in agreement and they said their fond farewells.

Ours was less demonstrative. "So long."

"Yeah. I'll be in touch."

I washed the coffeemaker, filling it with water and fresh coffee, ready for a quick fix whenever necessary. I started to put the mugs in the sink, but there was no room. I sighed and took all the clean dishes out of the dishwasher so I could put all the dirty ones in. That made me notice the paw marks and dog hairs on the kitchen floor. That's one of the many things I hate about housework: one thing always leads to another. This led me to a broom and then a mop and, shortly, into a foul humor.

I was not a woman who got some sort of emotional fulfillment out of vacuuming and dusting and washing windows. I was not the type to simper "Golly gee! How everything simply sparkles! How truly wonderful it is when everything simply sparkles!" Maybe someday I'd get real Martha Stewart-y and put ribbons on the dust bunnies and make a mobile out of the dirty coffee spoons. But not in this life. Come to think of it, it hadn't done Martha a helluva lot of good in the long run, either.

By now Fargo was begging anxiously for his run, looking somewhat disturbed by this unusual spate of housekeeping. Thank God for a truly important reason not to extend my housecleaning chores beyond what I'd already done. Certainly the dog's welfare must come first.

I still avoided Race Point, not that I logically had any thoughts of finding another foot on the beach. I just was not ready to go back quite yet. So we strolled down to Atlantic Street and walked down the right-of-way to the beach on the bay side. No dogs allowed. But it was winter and who cared. It was low tide and Fargo ran in circles, herding little groups of sandpipers hither and yon across the flats. Then he chased a few seagulls in their game of tag where the gulls were always "it." He charged the gulls and the gulls dive-bombed him and I guess everyone was happy. I know I was.

It was sunny and fairly warm and nearly windless. I deliberately thought of pleasant things. Another couple of months and I could plant my annual petunias and tomatoes. That was about the extent of my gardening. Every year I swore I'd do more. This year I meant it. I really would do a better gardening job, maybe some cucumbers and zinnias. Hadn't I said that *last* year? Maybe I'd be a little more interested in gardening if I had someone special to tell me how delicious the tomatoes tasted or how lovely the zinnias were this year. I paused and turned to look out across the bay.

A cast of characters-past came to mind. There had been Ellen, who would have found the row of tomatoes crooked and in need of replanting. She had missed her calling. She'd have made a perfect puppeteer. And Gail, who would have wanted to pick a tomato but could never decide which one. She would have been a perfect puppet. Why do these people never seem to get together?

About that time, I got the puppy Fargo, followed by Nancy. Who would have smiled enigmatically, picked the biggest tomato and looked sexy as hell, standing there eating it. I had innocently thought all was well. She liked the puppy and God knows, she was madly in love . . . unfortunately, it was with Nancy. Then along came Judy, who would have asked, "What tomatoes?" She adored the puppy—along with several other women. But I liked her. We were still friends. I kicked a small stone along the sand. Was this retrospective necessary?

And, my last duchess, Michelle, who would have weeded carefully, never a foot away from me, and always made sure I knew Fargo was lying in the zinnias. We stayed together perhaps longer than we should have, simply because neither of us wanted to admit defeat . . . and maybe wouldn't have needed to. But then a friend threw herself a small birthday party. I had perhaps a bourbon or two more than was wise and was playing the raconteur, entertaining the group with my *Tales of Fargo*. Michelle came up beside me with a big phony smile and advised my audience, "You know, I think she loves that dog more than she loves me."

Without a second thought, the bourbon replied, "And why would I not?" The room went silent. The party broke up shortly and so, of course, did we.

And so I was single. Well, it wasn't so bad. I didn't have to revise my housekeeping habits. I could grow tomatoes for myself if I really wanted to. I've had worse dates than Fargo for New Year's Eve. And I had good friends and family and plenty to keep me busy.

That reminded me, one day soon I'd have to spend a little time on my spring trip to Boston, making nice with the insurance people who supported my lavish lifestyle, just to remind them I was alive and well and on the side of justice . . . at least as they saw it.

Next month would be time to refinish my deck. About that time you'd start to hear hammers and saws and smell fresh paint all over town, as Provincetown put on her seasonal makeup and got ready to swing her beaded bag for the tourists.

The tourists would spring up like crocuses. Today you'd see one or two, tomorrow a hundred, next week a town full. All the gift shops and clothing stores would open up and spread their wares. I often wondered just how many T-shirts were actually sold in a season—probably in the millions. The "art" galleries would open all along Commercial Street, with hundreds of unbelievably trashy prints and garish paintings that looked like they'd been done by the numbers. There were galleries with good painters, like my friend Shari, who was actually making a pretty solid reputation for herself, but they were few.

The hotdog stands would open up along MacMillan Wharf, and people wearing the ubiquitous T-shirts and sandals and white socks and baggy shorts flapping against bony knees would stand about dripping mustard. The music stores would blare hard metal rock and brain numbing rap. Parents would scream at kids and each other. And gay couples who wouldn't dream of holding hands on their own couch would do so as they walked along the street, just because it was Provincetown and they enjoyed "going public."

The clubs got going around nine at night with young singers and groups hoping for a big-time break, tired old-timers despairing of any break at all and no-talents hoping their jobs would just last through the weekend. Customers fought their way inside, seated six-to-a-table that wasn't big enough for two, screaming to be heard a foot away, waving futilely for a waiter. The ear-splitting sounds from one club would spill over into those of another until it seemed the whole length of Commercial Street was one long cacophony.

It was a madhouse. And I loved it.

I sniffed the air. It was still cold and clean. The beach was still empty. The only sounds now were mews from the gulls and that beautiful deep bark from Fargo and the patient lap-lap of the bay. But it was coming. I could feel it. And I would welcome it with the same love/hate ambivalence that Fargo felt for the gulls. They were his entertainment and his challenge and his recreation, but—oh—he'd love to get his paws on just one!

He came up to me, wet halfway up his legs, tongue lolling.

"Ready to go?" He shook himself and tried to rub against me to dry off, but I dodged him. "You look thirsty," I added. "So am I, and our trusty Wharf Rat Bar is only a block or two away." I put his leash back on and—with my failed relationships strung out behind us like an untidy scarf of seaweed along the waterline—we headed for refreshment.

I tied Fargo to a rather large anchor tilted just outside the door where he could snooze away a placid, sun-warmed hour while I knocked back a cold one or two and put a finger on the town's pulse. It was probably throbbing fast and furious with news of the mysterious foot.

"Hello, Joseph!" I called as I walked through the door.

"Call me Joseph and I'll call you Alexandra," he replied with a grin. I asked him for a paper cup of water for the dog and took it outside. Returning, I picked up the Bud he had placed on the bar, paid him and went to my familiar table in back, across from the bar. Joe followed me over and gave the table a swipe with his bar towel as an excuse for being there. "Cops were in earlier, asking if anybody'd seen some Spanish looking fella with a mustache or anybody talking about a boat where it didn't ought to be. You know what's up?"

28

"Oh, I think it was just some kids from up around Orleans took a boat for an impromptu joyride or something," I lied. "I don't think Cuba has invaded yet."

"By this time of year, I almost wish they would invade—if they've got some American dollars, that is."

"I was just on the beach with some similar thoughts," I pouted at him. "You needn't remind me it's that lean time of year. Anything new and juicy?"

"You know that better'n anybody," he replied. "You're the one who found the foot."

"Yeah, lucky me."

"Well," he nodded toward the front of the building. "You've sure given that bunch of losers a whole new reason to call Ptown the drug capital of the world. Which nobody needed. Every fishing boat already thinks every other one is running drugs. The gang at the front table got all excited yesterday when two guys in business suits came in, ab-so-lute-ly sure they were DEA or FBI." He grinned bitterly. "Know who they were?"

"No."

"Mortician equipment salesmen. They'd made a sales call at Collins Funeral Home and it got to be lunch time. Charlie Collins told them we made good stuffed clams, so they came over here to give us a try. DEA! FBI! Hah." He nodded toward a group of grizzled fishermen nursing beers and shots. "Little formaldehyde is about what they need."

I laughed. Joe gave the table another little rub and went back to the bar. I sipped my beer and slowly the conversation from the other table began to penetrate my consciousness. I heard one of the men say, "But, Harmon, they told Joe they was funeral home salesmen."

"That were just a clever cover-up." Harmon answered. "They was dressed too sharp to be funeral home salesmen. Funeral people, they always wear them black or dark grey suits and ties. These men was way too spiffy. And young. Funeral people ain't never young."

"Sure they are, Harmon. Hell, Charlie Collins was young hisself when he started working for his daddy."

"Wel-l-ll, he didn't never *look* young. Anyways, I left not long after those men did, and when I got up to the street they was standin' outside their car lookin' at a map. Now *that* oughta tell you something in itself! So, I just walked right up to them and gave my name and informed them that I knew for certain that the *Ocean Pearl* and the *Katie Ann* was a-meetin' with a mothership out in the Atlantic and bringing in drugs. And while I hoped they wouldn't spread it around who told 'em, I thought they ought to take some fast action to put a stop to it. Yes, I did! And you know what they said to me?"

The men at the table—and I—leanly expectantly toward Harmon's answer.

"Well, sir, the kinda fat one, he looks at me for a long minute, like he's deciding if he c'n trust me. Then he says, real solemn-like, 'Sir, we appreciate your civic spirit. We won't tell nobody what you told us, and we will certainly take it under ad-ad-advisement.' Them was his very words." Harmon nodded sharply as if he had proven his point beyond further debate, and I began to get that need of fresh air feeling. I drained my beer and was about to stand.

And she walked through the door.

# Chapter 4

I watched her as she paused in the doorway to let her eyes adjust
to the watery light admitted by the Wharf Rat's salt-sprayed
windows. With hands in pockets and collar turned up against the
outdoor chill, she had a young and somewhat vulnerable look. I
pegged her at twenty-five, no more. Her hair was dark and curly, cut
short against a well-formed head. A straight, rather narrow nose
topped a mouth that looked as if it could smile easily. Her eyes were
a warm brown, her skin fair. She wasn't terribly tall, maybe five-five
or so. But the straight-cut jeans held long dancer's legs. I knew
underneath the soft denim would be muscular calves and smooth
elongated thighs ending in small solid buttocks that would be the
perfect handhold. As she removed her jacket, the high, round little
breasts nudged her sweater as if reminding it to touch them gently.

She took a seat about a third of the way down the bar, and Joe
was there with a smiling swiftness he rarely showed to his regular

customers, polishing the portion of the bar in front of her with a surprisingly clean bar cloth and unusual promptitude. They spoke briefly and Joe actually provided her not only with a coaster but a cocktail napkin and dish of peanuts before leaving to fill her order.

I smiled to myself. Joe would give it his best try, and it wouldn't be good enough. It often was. He wasn't bad looking and he had a certain sardonic charm that worked quite well, not only with some of the local ladies, but tourists as well. Of course, most of Joe's flirtatious efforts were carried on with the safety of a chest-high bar between him and his prey. There were lots of meaningful looks and double entendres, but Joe was ever mindful that if he developed a zipper problem, his wife Billie would throttle him.

But his magic wouldn't work this time. She was gay. Sometimes you simply knew, and this was one of those times.

And, I reminded myself, *faint heart ne'er won fair maiden*. I ran my fingers through my own short hair, straightened my jacket and walked to the bar. "Hello." I extended my hand. "I'm Alex Peres, mind if I sit down?"

She favored me with a small, tight smile and a brief, firm handshake. "I'm Janet Meacham. Do sit down." She stared the length of the empty bar. "It's so crowded in here. You're very lucky this one stool was left vacant."

Ouch. I quickly ran down my collection of swift and clever replies and didn't seem to find one that fit that particular remark. I settled on being the harmless and sincere local yokel. "Well, I'll agree with being lucky anyway. No intention of bothering you, it's just that I've never seen you around before and thought I'd do my part as a Chamber of Commerce member in good standing and say welcome. If you'd rather be alone I'll just quietly disappear and cry myself to sleep."

Joe arrived with what looked like a vodka tonic, setting it down with a flourish for her and a nasty look for me. I ordered a bourbon and water before he could disappear, or she could dismiss me, and slid onto the stool. She took a sip of the drink and turned toward me. "I apologize. You're being friendly and I'm being beastly. Let's start all over again. Yes, I'm new in town, as of a couple of days ago. I take it you are not. New in town, I mean."

"Native, in fact. I've been here most of my life."

"What's kept you in one place, aside from your Chamber of Commerce duties, of course?" This time her smile looked real.

I rarely tell people when I first meet them that I'm a private investigator. It seems either to intimidate or slyly amuse them, and both reactions irritate me. So I told her my almost-true version. "I'm a nature photographer, and I've yet to find a better spot to be one. Where's your spot?"

"Oh," she laughed, "I'm more like a Dalmatian. Maybe not a quite hundred-and-one spots, but close. Originally New Hampshire, bounced around all over the place in the Coast Guard for several years, then Boston." Here her voice changed, and her eyes were both sad and wary. "I - I just got out of a bad relationship, and Boston suddenly seemed loaded with all those old familiar places and faces you really don't want to see right now. It was change of scenery time. I've always thought I might want to give writing a try, and Provincetown off-season seemed a nice, quiet place to start. Or at least try to start."

"You're in pretty good company. Eugene O'Neill and Norman Mailer gave us an A-plus reference. Have you found your garret yet?"

"Garret?" Then she picked up on my erudite humor. "Oh, yes. I rented a small studio. Actually it's half of a two-car garage made into an apartment over on Mather Street. The landlady is an absolute darling named Mrs. Madeiros. The place is clean and simple and cheap, which is about what I'm up to right now."

"Understood. Well, just as part of my Chamber of Commerce responsibilities, you understand, how about having lunch with me tomorrow? I have to deliver some photos up to a fairly interesting art gallery in Wellfleet, and I know a pretty good restaurant there. You might enjoy both. What say you?"

33

"Oh, I'm sure it would be lovely, but I really think . . ." What sounded like an impending refusal was cut off by the noisy arrival of my dear brother.

Sonny opened the door, stood framed in it for a second, and closed it with definite firmness. I must admit as a detective sergeant he looked impressive. He was in uniform, which was unusual, and probably meant he was covering for another officer who was sick or on vacation. He stood there in full police regalia complete to peaked officer's cap, hip holster, radio clipped to his belt, perfectly creased trousers and those very unofficial black shiny boots. Everyone in the place looked up, including Janet, whose face reflected curiosity and just a tinge of unease.

It's funny how so many people see a cop and immediately get a guilty expression. I suppose it's simply that we all are guilty of this or that—parking by the fireplug, swiping an apple off a fruit stand, dinging a car in a parking lot and not reporting it—and we automatically figure that somehow the cop knows! Whatever Janet's and my particular sins may have been, Sonny's interest was not in us at that moment. He walked right past us to the table of men at the front.

"Harmon," he said sadly, "You've left the lights on in that wreck you call a truck . . . again! You'll be out there begging patrol cars for a jump start in an hour and, believe it or not, once in awhile they have other things to do. Now be a good guy and go turn'em off and run that so-called vee-hicle till it charges."

Harmon jumped to his feet. "Oh, gosh. Thanks for telling me, Sonny. I'm sorry, I really am. I woulda swore I turned them lights off when I came in. I'll go and take care of it right away. And I won't bother none of the patrolmen."

"Harmon," Sonny asked patiently, "Why do you run with your lights on in the middle of the day?"

"I heard on the TV it's safer, like people can see you coming better."

"They can hear you coming a mile away in that damn thing!" The men at the table laughed and Harmon glared, as Sonny continued.

34

"Harmon, some new cars come with daytime running lights. I do not believe the word 'new' applies to your truck. Those of us who do not have vee-hicles equipped with running lights put on our lights in rain, fog, snow. We put 'em on at dusk and dawn and in mountains where there's deep shadow all day. We do not put them on in downtown Provincetown in broad daylight and then forget to turn them off when we park! Do we?"

"Sure, I mean no. Thanks, Sonny. Say, c'n I buy you a drink?"

"Harmon," Sonny answered wearily, "That's extremely safe generosity. You know I can't drink in uniform."

"Well, I'll owe you one," he said quickly. He turned toward the door.

Sonny let him open the door and then called out, "Hey, Harmon, tell you what, I'll tell Joe to charge one to your tab and I'll come back and have it later. Okay?" Harmon looked stricken and scuttled out the door, borne on gales of laughter from his cronies. Sonny smiled sourly. "Reckon he'd about die if I did it."

"I reckon so would Joe about die if you did it," I smiled, as he walked toward Janet and me. "Harmon's tab is probably about equal to the national debt as it is. But let me mind my manners. Janet Meacham, my brother, Sonny Pcres." I watched as Sonny took her hand and said hello. But his gaydar was better than Joe's. Sonny was pleasant, but he didn't bother to turn on the thousand-watt Peres charm. I was doing that.

Still, when Sonny turned back to me, he was obviously in high good humor. "Well, Alex, you lose the bet. You owe me a nice, rare steak."

"I don't remember betting you a steak. What are you talking about?"

"The boat. I was right, there was a twenty-eight foot Bertram cruiser stolen from the boatyard the night of the storm. The robbery."

"Oh, boy," I mused. "They could be just about anywhere by now, short of Europe—that's a good, solid little boat. It would weather most any storm if they knew how to handle it."

"Unfortunately for them, apparently they didn't. The Coast Guard had choppers out looking for them early this morning, and one of them spotted some debris on the water. They sent a cutter out and she picked up some stuff still floating around. There were a couple of cushions with the boat's name stenciled on them and a cooler that the owner identified as having been on the boat. It's certainly probable that she sank, and I assume that's how your foot got separated from its owner."

"Dammit! It's not *my* foot and I wish . . ." I began. Then I happened to glance at Janet. She was looking at us with that totally bemused expression of someone who has joined a conversation in *medias res* and has absolutely no inkling of what anyone is talking about.

"I'm sorry, Janet, we're being rude. Let me fill you in. You see, Monday night there was a robbery and murder over in Plymouth, and the robbers apparently stole this boat in their escape . . . but it seems they had some bad luck with it. Anyway, on Tuesday I was running my dog on the beach, and he found this sneaker that still had a man's foot inside it. We figure he fell overboard somehow and caught his foot in the propeller and . . ."

She never said a word. She didn't try to hold on to anything. She just keeled over. Fortunately, Sonny was faster than I was. He pulled her back against his chest to support her, or she'd have fallen off the bar stool and been lying on the dubiously cleaned floorboards of the Wharf Rat Bar.

"Congratulations, Alex, you really know how to grab your audience." Sonny raised his voice. "Joe! We need some brandy down here, right now!"

Brandy! I thought. The Wharf Rat probably hadn't sold brandy since it sold bathtub gin. But I was wrong. Joe fished and rattled around among some bottles and came up with one that at least *said* Brandy on the label. In keeping with the Rat's long tradition of first class service, he slopped a couple of ounces into a beer glass and gave it a shuffleboard spin down the bar, where I caught it before it slid past us onto the floor. Obviously Joe's interest in Janet was waning fast.

She was conscious, but white and confused, still leaning heavily against Sonny. I put the glass to her lips and she took a swallow. At that point her eyes flew wide open and she straightened up as if galvanized. "My *God*!" She gasped. "What *is* that?"

Paint thinner would have been my immediate answer, but I simply murmured soothingly and Sonny released his grip and patted her on the shoulder. It occurred to me that Joe might have a great medical miracle here. He could probably use his brandy to pull people out of deep comas. Janet certainly seemed alert, if still shaky.

I began to apologize, but she put up her hand and shook her head. "It's me," she said. "I have the world's weakest stomach. Please, I'm the one who's sorry for causing all the ruckus. Please, go ahead with your story."

Sonny took over, speaking slowly, choosing his words carefully. "There doesn't seem to be much more to tell. The Plymouth police figure that the boat went down in the storm, the two robbers went down with it and drowned, and that's the end of that."

"And the Plymouth police don't think the real owner of the boat was involved with the robbers?" I asked.

"No." Sonny gave that funny little giggle that told me he was truly amused. "For one thing, the owners are a Plymouth couple who are filthy rich, and it's old family money. The family has lived in Plymouth for literally centuries, and they didn't suddenly get mysteriously rich in the last couple of years or something, like it might be drugs. They go all the way back to the Mayflower's original passenger list and they both have an alibi that's too crazy to be anything but true."

I saw his eyes glinting and knew he was dying to recount it, so, being a good guy, I fed him his line. "What sort of alibi?"

"They were going out Monday night to some hundred-dollar-a-drink-benefit. You will recall it was sleeting at the time. But off they started anyway, in their fancy tux and long dress. Mr. McKinney had on new shoes and slipped on his top step. Ended up in a heap at the bottom with a broken ankle. The wife and the next-door neighbor got him into the car and off to the hospital. He gets a cast and some crutches and they bring him home."

Already smiling, Janet and I both chuckled aloud as Sonny went into the awkward antics of a man, unfamiliar with crutches, trying to climb stairs.

"He's hobbling up the front stairs, when his darling wife runs up the steps in front of him to open the door. Somehow he puts a crutch down on her foot. She screams and yanks her foot out from under. He goes *back* down the steps and cracks a bone in his wrist. Mrs. McKinney has two broken toes. They are now both resting comfortably at home."

By now Janet and I were laughing and wiping our eyes. "And when is the divorce?" Janet finally managed to ask.

"No divorce," I answered. "The next-door neighbor shot them both and put them out of their misery."

"Janet may just be right," Sonny grinned widely. "The Plymouth detective who talked with them said the air had a definite chill to it. But through his gritted teeth the owner did remember one thing that makes me wonder why Plymouth is so ready to call it a done deal."

"What's that?" I asked.

"The Bertram carried a Zodiac with a high-powered outboard."

"A Zodiac?" Janet looked confused. "You mean like an astrology chart?"

"No," Sonny explained. "It's the Cadillac of inflatable boats. It's virtually unsinkable, with several separate air chambers and a very tough hide. It can carry an extremely powerful motor and live through just about anything if it's handled correctly."

"Aye, there's the rub, though," I said. "Once again—was it handled right? It looks like the cruiser definitely went down. At least one of them was overboard and . . . er, badly hurt at some point . . . and, ah . . . indications are it was probably the bigger guy. Could the smaller man have managed to handle things alone after the big guy was . . . no longer available? He would have had to be really good at it."

"I know. You're probably right. I just don't like loose ends. Anyway, I've got to get going. Nice to have met you, Janet. See you around, Alex."

"Thanks for the rescue and first aid," Janet called after him. He waved without looking back and went out the door.

"Lord," Janet said, "Is life in Provincetown always this exciting?"

"About once in every thirty years. We had a serial killer back in the seventies."

"Don't say another word! I can't deal with more of that rare old brandy, however well intentioned you may be. And I have to get going, too." She stood and reached for her jacket. "But about lunch tomorrow . . . is the offer still open after my sad performance thus far? Can a lady change her mind?"

I had no idea what had spurred her to accept my invitation. Maybe her near-death experience with the brandy made her realize what a charming companion I really am. "Absolutely. How about I pick you up at your apartment around eleven-thirty? I know where it is—I've known Mrs. Madeiros since my trick-or-treat days."

She agreed and we walked outside and I noticed Janet look up at the almost twilight sky—the automatic reaction of the pilot, the farmer, the sailor—and I recalled she was one of the three. For no reason at all I saw us together in a sailboat on a gentle moonlit sea.

I blinked and the image disappeared as Janet said goodnight and walked on up the alley toward Commercial Street. I stopped to untie Fargo, who was stretching and yawning mightily. We just had time to get home and find something to eat before we piled into the car and went on our nightly safari to track the anything-but-elusive Ray Miller.

Miller left his home right on schedule after dinner and drove downtown. He parked, went into his building, and the second floor lights came on as usual. But this time he must actually have had work to do, for he did not come back out. A couple of times I saw shadows moving behind the upstairs blinds and assumed he was really there, and there seemed to be only one figure. I was bored. Bored and cold. Bored and cold and sleepy.

I gave Fargo a drink and me some coffee. I thought about Janet. She seemed bright and nice. She was certainly attractive. My latest bout of celibacy seemed now to have been a long, long time. Sharing a bed with Fargo was warm and pleasant and—sorry, my pet—predictable. I wondered if Janet were ready for an affair. How long had she been apart from her last lover? It didn't sound as if it had been long, and although I could definitely be interested, I had no desire to take advantage of her possible vulnerability. I didn't much like people who did that. Well, we'd see how things went.

I'd bet her hair was soft to touch. Now where did *that* come from?

I had been 'single' since last fall—God, had it been *that* long?—but wondered if I really wanted a casual affair? Of late I had been thinking that permanency might hold charms I had never explored.

Of course the operative word there was still "might." Permanency didn't seem to work too well for me. I wanted a partner, but I sure hadn't had much luck in choosing one. It seemed that the very qualities which attracted me to a woman all too shortly became the ones that caused trouble.

I ground my cigarette out rather aggressively. With the exception of Nancy who, I had heard, had taken her solipsistic cocoon out to the fertile hunting ground of San Diego—my choices hadn't really been so bad. I shouldn't be so gun-shy.

Stiffness was setting in. I needed to move. I hooked on Fargo's lead, figuring that Miller wouldn't be going anywhere in the next three minutes. While Fargo looked for the right bush, I wondered if one of the affairs might have turned permanent if I had simply set some parameters.

Fargo and I returned to the car to see Miller's office lights wink out. He walked down to the Guv and went in. This guy would drink anywhere. I kept an eye on the Guv's door in my rear view window, and continued my threnody. I tended to avoid personal issues and simply withdrew. This resulted in my lovers' complaints that I was aloof or cool or unreachable or even—the one accusation I could righteously deny—unfaithful.

But there were times I craved solitude like an alcoholic needs booze. And people who don't need it tend not to understand those who do. Even so, I could hardly say the ladies-past were entirely to blame. Sometimes I saw a bit of my father in me, and I didn't like it.

Over the years I had thought I was emotionally unmarked by break-ups, whether I had been the dumper or dumpee, or whether the relationship had simply withered away. Now I wondered. I was attracted to Janet. I was afraid of being attracted to Janet. I didn't want another merry mix-up. If I got involved, I wanted it to work, dammit!

I lit my eighth cigarette of the day and dared Fargo to open his mouth.

I wanted someone to do things with. Or do nothing with. Or enjoy telling each other about the things we had done separately. To grow the damn tomatoes with. God, was that so much? Wasn't it possible to be permanent without being joined at the hip?

Of course, it took a similarly minded partner for that to work. I tried to remember the comment I'd read that Jessica Tandy had made when some reporter asked her how she and Hume Cronin had lasted so long, something about separate bedrooms, separate bathrooms and separate checkbooks. My mind drifted off into ways to accomplish the first two requisites by remodeling my house. I was deep into bigger and bigger architectural changes, dreaming of second floors with two-bedroom, two-bathroom master suites—maybe a balcony . . .

I almost screamed aloud at the black apparition suddenly blocking my window. Then I realized that Fargo hadn't barked and that his tail was thumping the back of the seat. It was Sonny.

"Sweet Jesus in the foothills! You scared me to death!"

"I thought you were asleep or passed out or something. What the hell are you doing parked down here at ten o'clock?"

"Doing a little checking on Ray Miller. His wife thinks he's playing around and wants to find out who else is in the game, but thus far all I've seen is a couple of nights drinking with a couple of the boys from the bank. And tonight he seemed to be legitimately working and is now night-capping at the Guv. Unless, of course, the bankers are gay and he really is *playing* with the boys."

Sonny reached in and took my cigarettes off the dashboard. "No. He's straight. But he is playing around . . . with Marcia Robby. Usually on Thursday nights at her place. Well, I guess it would hardly be *his* place, would it?" He laughed. "Go home, Alex. You look beat. If you're going to keep up with that infant you were ready to devour in one bite, you'll need your rest."

I took the lighter and pack out of his hand. "Good night, Sonny."

I was more irritated than beat. I didn't like the crack about my age. So Janet was maybe eight years younger than I. That was hardly a generation gap. And she'd been around. She seemed pretty sophisticated.

I started the car, suddenly in a foul mood. Here I'd stayed up for three nights, frozen and bored watching Miller, and Sonny knew the whole story all along. I guess there isn't much cops in a small town don't know. And I couldn't imagine what got into me to tell Sonny why I was parked downtown. Not that he would care, or say anything to anyone, but I never discussed a local client, even with Sonny. If I hadn't been lost in some romantic daydream I wouldn't have let it slip. Dammit! I didn't usually let my personal life overlap into my professional one.

The hell with Miller this night! I drove home, and Fargo and I lost no time in climbing wearily into bed. As I drifted off, I reached out and stroked his silky ear. "Fargo, if we need to share for a while, we'll get a bigger bed at least, until we can do something with the house. You won't have to sleep on the floor, don't worry." He pulled his head away and I could feel his dirty look.

*"Share? Floor?"*

42

# Chapter 5

I was up early Thursday morning and in high good humor.

I had a date. Well, come on now, it had been a while! Fargo caught my good spirits and kept grinning and nudging my elbow while I tried to drink my first cup of coffee and have that first cigarette that always tastes so good you forget all about the people who tell you how bad you are.

Ever the strict disciplinarian, I made him wait all of three minutes before I put on my down jacket and snapped on his leash and we began our walk down to Atlantic Street and the bayside beach. Race Point still wasn't calling out to me.

As we walked along Commercial Street, a blue van came toward us. I thought it looked familiar, and then I recognized the family from New Jersey who had been at Race Point on the fateful Day of the Foot. I waved cheerily, but the adults didn't seem to see me. They seemed fascinated by something on the other side of the street, although I couldn't see what. I thought the van speeded up, and the children stared moon-eyed out the back window and the little girl may have waggled her fingers a bit.

At the beach I took off Fargo's leash, and he bounded away into his on-going war of the seagulls. I followed him more sedately, enjoying the crisp morning with its promise of sun and tantalizing hint of spring warmth. Something was bouncing around in the back of my mind. You know how it is when someone has said something that later kind of clangs in your brain as being wrong, but you don't really pick up on it at the time and later can't remember what it is?

Someone had said something that didn't add up, or rang false . . . or something. Had it been Sonny? Or Janet? Maybe even something silly old Harmon had said? God, how I hate it when that happens! I tried not to think about it, as that usually works best in making it come to the surface, but apparently not this morning.

My mental machinations were interrupted by a deep woof from Fargo down the beach. I jumped as if I'd been plugged in with the toaster. Dear God, not another foot! No, of course not. Just a little dachshund, running circles and darting between Fargo's legs in that pointless frenzy that dachshunds seem to find so entertaining. I let them play for a while, then leashed Fargo again and started home. I had places to go and things to do. The beady-eyed little guy seemed disappointed that the game had ended, but finally trotted off toward one of the bed and breakfasts located along the beach.

Meanwhile, back at the ranch, with the thought that Janet might—just *might*—come back with me after lunch, I quickly went around taking shirts and jackets off door knobs and consigning them to washer or closet. I ran a dust cloth over the most obvious surfaces, took out trash and papers, put dishes in the dishwasher and turned it on and closed the door to the office/workroom. So much for housecleaning. Anyway, I had done that kitchen floor the day before, hadn't I? Finally, I changed the bed. Well, you can never tell. You might get lucky. If you don't, you've got a nice clean bed to feel lonely in.

After my shower, I dried my hair and dressed rather formally for me, selecting a white cowl-neck sweater and navy flannel slacks. I even added a single strand of pearls to the outfit and got out my trusty camel's hair topcoat instead of my usual L. L. Bean all-weather jacket.

Fargo watched these I-am-going-out-and-you-can't-come-with-me actions with ever-deepening sadness, finally disappearing entirely under the bed and refusing to come out, even to get the biscuits I left for his consolation while I was gone. Telling myself I had absolutely no reason to feel guilty, I picked up the pictures for Jay's gallery, called a spuriously cheery, "I won't be long! Now you be a good boy!" in the general direction of the bed, and left. Feeling, of course, terribly guilty.

I was on time to the minute, when I reached Mrs. Madeiros' house. Don't think I was eager or anything. As I started up the driveway, Janet waved from the big front window, obviously putting on a jacket. When she came out, she looked absolutely stunning in dark charcoal brown slacks, a burnt orange turtleneck and a brown tweed blazer that didn't seem warm enough for the weather. She was walking fast in the chilly air.

I turned back to the car, opened the passenger door for her and then went around to my side. She got quickly into the car and shivered once, putting her hands out to the heater. "Brrr! I always seem to forget March is still wintertime! Winter should end with February, shouldn't it?" She turned and smiled at me, and I found it very easy to smile back.

"If not January," I answered. I turned toward Route 6. "Hungry?"

'Working on it. What's the drill?"

"Nothing special." I indicated the canvas bag on the back seat. "We'll drop the photos off at Jay's gallery, which you'll probably enjoy. He has some nice stuff. Frankly, I think a lot of it is pretty pricey. But at some point in your young life, if you like, you may want to try and pick up a Shari Mittenthal there. She's not really well-known and so she's not awfully expensive yet, but I think some-

45

day she will be. Get something that has a fence in it, fences are starting to be her trademark."

"That would be great. I've never had anything by an 'undiscovered' artist who later became famous. In fact, I don't think I've ever owned an original. Wouldn't it be fun, years later at a really posh party in your penthouse, to say casually to admirers, 'Oh, yes, it's an early Mittenthal. I realized simply years ago on Cape Cod she'd someday be very, ah . . . worthwhile.'"

"Meow. You're not nice." I laughed.

"Of course I am. That's just a fantasy, I'm really nice. Well, usually nice. Uh, sort of nice."

"We'd better quit while we're ahead."

We drove past the dunes, which for some reason reminded Janet of sleeping elephants, she said. We went by the rows and rows of boarded up cottages and motels along Beach Point. More than the leafless trees, the grey sand grasses or the lack of traffic, these closed up little buildings with their gaily painted trim and their optimistic signs of *Beach-front Rooms & Cottages!* and *Low Weekly Rates!* and *Some Units With Kitchens!* calling out to empty parking lots made me know the winter was still with us.

When they had cars and vans in the front yards, and towels and bathing suits on the clothes lines, with coveys of small children on the swings and slides centered on the lawns, and the smell of grilling food permeating the air along the two-mile strip, then I would know that summer had well and truly returned. We passed Truro, finally turning off on the road down to Wellfleet harbor. I coasted to a stop in front of Jay's Art Gallery.

Janet helped me carry one of the bags of photos in and then looked around the gallery while Jay and I completed our business. True to form, Jay admired all the photos spread out on the backroom table, then picked up three, held them out to me with an apologetic moue, murmuring, "These are lovely, too, Alex, but somehow I just don't get the feel they're quite *us.*"

I shrugged mentally and took them from him. I found them little different from the others, and there was no *us*. Jay was never attached to anyone for longer than the eleven o'clock news. But he then handed me a check for a sizable amount for photos he had sold over the winter and told me to check with him the end of April, when he was expecting the season to pick up and would need "a goodly number" of photos for the summer. What the hell, I thought, we all have our little foibles.

"See anything you like?" I asked Janet as I walked back into the gallery.

"Oh, yes. Very much so. You're right about Mittenthal, there's one—complete with fence—I really love, but right now . . ."

"Yeah, I know. I've learned to leave my checkbook home when I come here. Let me just put these pictures in the car and we'll eat." I wondered how Janet was fixed for money, and told myself to be sure I got the lunch check.

We walked down the block to Separate Tables, a big old Victorian-style house that had been converted into a restaurant. The owners had been clever, I thought, by leaving the original design of the downstairs alone instead of knocking out walls to make one large dining room. You had a choice of dining in several rather small rooms: the library, the parlor, the dining room or the sun room. The library was the bar, complete with books.

We had a drink in the library and moved on to the sun room, which was warm and bright in the early afternoon. It overlooked a small garden. In the summer, I knew, it would be charming, but now it was a uniform wintry grey, with an empty, leaf-strewn fountain and some small statues of animals scattered about looking cold and forlorn. I was glad Janet's chair faced inward, toward some charming and colorful familiar impressionist prints.

After an appetizer of Wellfleet oysters, the waiter brought around the wine list while we waited for our entree. I'm no oenophile. Personally I like a nice claret with just about anything. But I thought I should try at least to choose a white wine to go with the seafood we had ordered. I skipped sauternes—they all taste like vinegar to me—and moved on to the chardonnays. I selected one about midway in the price list and hoped for the best.

They brought the bottle out with the usual absurd fanfare, showing me the label, proffering the cork and then pouring a bit from the towel-wrapped bottle into my glass. The waiter looked so haughty and patronizing, I felt I had no choice but to go into my wine-expert act. I squeezed the cork to make sure the tip was damp. At least I knew not to sniff it. I picked up the glass, whirled it around and sniffed that. Then I took a sip, squished it around in my mouth and finally swallowed.

"Aah, aa-aah," I pronounced solemnly, "A sturdy little wine, unpretentious, yet subtly aware of its true importance."

Janet literally let out a whoop of laughter that caused nearby heads to turn. She stifled her next outburst and wiped her eyes with her napkin. "You know you are certifiable, don't you? Sturdy little wine! How about impudent, yet captivating? Or delicate, with just a hint of inner strength?" She turned to the waiter and smiled. "I'm sure it's perfectly fine. Just pour, please." He did, looking as if he had sampled some of his vinegary sauternes.

A waitress was right behind him with our luncheons. I'd picked the local bay scallops with their wonderful nutty taste, and curly French-fried potatoes plus a fresh asparagus salad. Janet was having filet of sole *Veronique* and an endive with avocado salad. The meal was served with a crusty loaf of herb bread and sweet butter. And the wine, thank God, was indeed fine. We concentrated on the food for a while in companionable silence.

Then Janet asked how my scallops were. "Best in the world," I answered. "Caught right out here in the bay, probably early this morning. And well prepared, I might add."

"My sole is good, too."

"Probably caught in Miami, frozen for six months and flown in," I teased. "I never could understand sole *Veronique*. It is cast in stone that French-fries go with fish. Who eats grapes with fish?"

"Well, it's delicious," she defended. "And it's quite a historical dish. While your ancestors were still painting themselves blue, the Romans were dining on sole *Veronique*! Perhaps in some former life

48

I reclined on a couch beside the emperor and peeled him a grape. Then I dipped it in poisoned wine and fed it to him and became the all-powerful empress."

"Gee, you'd have been perfect as Mrs. Nero."

"Such a nasty, overrated little boy. I'd have had him for breakfast and then spit out the seeds."

"You *are* ferocious! Listen, Empress Veronique, if we should go into a time warp and find ourselves in ancient Rome, remind me to head for the provinces on the first ox cart express."

"I'd find you. And make you bring me here again for lunch. It's really perfect."

And she was really charming, I thought. I couldn't remember when I'd so enjoyed a luncheon. She may have been only twenty-five, but there was a worldliness about her that belied her youth.

She cut herself another small slice of bread and buttered it. "This herb bread is superb. I recognize the marjoram and rosemary, but I can't place the seeds. And that's unusual, I'm customarily pretty good at identifying tastes."

"I'm almost sure it's borage."

"Really? I'm not sure I've ever had it. You're very clever."

"It was a popular kitchen herb in England back in the fourteenth century, just as my ancestors were over in the creek scrubbing off the woad and putting on the shining armor. That's quite a while after we threw you Romans out. They used it in salads, as well as breads. And medicinally for something, too, but I can't remember what it was."

"Good grief! I've an expert on my hands! You must be a fabulous cook!"

"Oh, yes," I agreed. "I make an omelet that is simply beautiful until you try to get it out of the skillet. And I make a very tasty grilled cheese and tomato sandwich. The bread gets this really interesting dark brown, but somehow the cheese doesn't melt and the tomato falls out."

"Oh, come on!"

"About my cooking, it's the absolute truth. I do know a bit about herbs because of my Aunt Mae. When her husband died, she started fooling with herbs as kind of a hobby to take up her time. Now she's made quite a little cottage industry out of it." Janet gave me a curious look over the top of her wine glass. "She grows them in the backyard and sells them dried in bottles, or growing in those tiny clay pots. She has a bunch of tourists who come back to her place year after year. In fact she's written two little books about them, and they actually sell well enough to stay in print. You know, in nature food shops or gift shops, and a few little specialty book stores around New England."

Janet was obviously impressed. "That's fascinating! I love to cook, and I love herbs, properly used. I've always wanted my own restaurant, a small one with my own unique touch." Her eyes lit up just thinking about it. "Maybe I'll call it The Veronique. One where I could meet the diners and yet do some cooking, too. Intimate, I guess that's the word I'm looking for. But not kitschy."

"Oh, never kitschy," I smiled. "But you are going to be one busy lady—a book here, a restaurant there . . ."

She looked down, embarrassed, and I was immediately sorry I had teased her about it. She reddened but she answered stoutly, "Well, I guess I'll just have to be an overachiever!"

We went on to finish our meal and coffee, chatting about nothing in particular. Teachers we had liked or disliked. Food we like or dislike. Movies, books. Places we had been. She told me about her time out in Washington State where she had been stationed while in the Coast Guard. She had loved it. Especially out on the Olympic Peninsula just west of Seattle. She rhapsodized over the mountains, the lakes, America's only tropical rain forest, and the silent beauty of the Pacific with the stone monoliths rising eerily from its quiet surface on a foggy day. She showed me a snapshot of her, standing in front of a shining glacier, in sun so warm she wore short sleeves, and with three lovely, tiny mountain deer browsing at ease, not twenty feet from her. Her face had a lovely glow to it, and I wondered if the gleam was for Seattle or maybe just a little for me.

"I've never been there, of course," I said. "But you're making that sound like something I should remedy. And probably sooner rather than later. It sounds magnificent. But I tend to get lost easily. I'd definitely need a guide. Any idea where I could find a good one?"

"I was a Girl Scout. We never get lost. We make very reliable guides. In fact we double as two-legged St. Bernards." She smiled at me and our eyes met in one of those glances that seems marvelously promising as it occurs, and may or may not have been caused by the wine, and may or may not mean a damned thing an hour from now.

We were getting to know each other, I realized, and it felt rather nice. Janet might be seven or eight years younger than I was, but it didn't seem to affect the pleasure we were taking in each other's company. Screw Sonny.

Then the haughty waiter was clearing his throat and looking sauterne-y again and it dawned on me that we had been there quite a long while. I got the check. We argued over it but I finally won, and we left.

On the way back to the car we stopped in a small bookshop that was new to me and, of course, to Janet. We separated to browse. I soon picked up the latest Rita Mae Brown mystery and took it up to the register. After I paid for it, I leaned against the counter to read the first few pages while I waited for Janet. It looked like she might be a while, but then she hurried over to me, eyes shining, holding up two little brightly colored paperbacks.

"Look here!" she cried. "Two herb books by a Mac Cartwright! They must be your Aunt Mae's books, aren't they? Isn't that great? I'm going to get them. Could you possibly get her to sign them for me?"

"Sure. They're hers, and I know she'd be delighted. Of the few authors I've met, I've yet to see one who wouldn't walk a mile in a driving snowstorm to autograph a book."

"How right you are!" The store owner came to life. "Once in awhile we have a book signing here, and the authors will write special little messages and sign their names on the flyleaf until their fingers are frozen to the pen—with nary a groan. They don't even take a bathroom break, for fear they might miss someone."

Janet managed to catch one of the books in the strap of her purse. Both books and purse fell to the floor. Typical stuff flew all over the place: tissues, comb, compact, pens, scraps of paper, lipstick, wallet . . . you name it. I scooped several papers, pens and the wallet together and picked them up. A driver's license fell out of the wallet as I lifted it and dropped back to the floor. As it landed, I noticed it was a Connecticut license, not Massachusetts, as I would have expected. She plucked it from the floor and the wallet from my hands and jammed them all quickly back into the purse, her face red with embarrassment.

"Isn't that silly of me, keeping that old expired Connecticut license all these years?" I was amused at her discomfiture. It made her seem very young again after the sophisticated woman I had seen at lunch.

"I have no idea why it is still in my wallet. Why, it must have been in there since I was stationed at New London! Lord knows it's worthless. Typical woman, huh? Maybe this will inspire me to clean out this bag and wallet." She smiled up at the owner. "I'm mortified at all this junk, although I suppose some of it might find a market as antique." She managed to come up with two $10 bills and hand them to the woman.

"Don't be mortified, my dear." The woman smiled as she put Janet's books into a bag and handed back her change. "I've only owned this store a few months, but you wouldn't believe some of the weird things I've seen come flying out of handbags and pockets in here! You wouldn't believe it, for the plain and simple reason I'd be too embarrassed to tell you!"

We all laughed. Janet finally had everything back in her purse and the books in hand, and we left. Driving back to Provincetown we chatted about Aunt Mae's books and the mystery I had bought. Janet didn't know Rita Mae Brown, and when I told her that two of the main characters were a Welsh Corgi named Tucker and a cat named Sneaky Pie, who talked to each other and to other animals, she laughed. "I'm not surprised. If you ever wrote a book I'm sure Fargo would be in it. Does he talk, like the ones in the book you bought?"

"I'm sure he talks to other animals in some manner. I've noticed that various barks and growls and whines seem to have a lot of different meanings. And even though he may not speak English, he very definitely manages to communicate most of what he wants to say to me, one way or another."

As we crested the last hill in Truro we looked down on Provincetown, curled up for a late afternoon nap by the harbor. The roofs of the buildings made a haphazard colorful quilt, bordered by the sand dunes turning a pale peach in the lowering rays of the sun. It was lovely and, unthinking, our hands reached out to each other.

We drove a few moments that way. I suddenly realized the day was nearly over, and I didn't want it to end. Or rather, I knew exactly how I wanted it to end. I just wasn't sure how to make that happen. So I decided to try something very original.

"Uh . . . ah, would you like to stop back by my place for a drink?"

She looked at me and grinned. "I thought you'd never ask."

I was awfully glad I had changed the bed.

# Chapter 6

I'm only speaking for myself, of course. But whenever a companion and I have decided to have sex together for the very first time, the moments between entering the bedroom and actually finding ourselves in bed are worse than any root canal on record. It's all a matter of logistics. That first time, how the hell do you go about getting undressed and into bed?

Do you A) Run around the room shedding clothes wherever they may fall and calling out, "I want you! I need you! I must have you now!"? B) Suddenly become *teddibly* British, saying, "With you in half a tick, Luv," and undress neatly, folding your clothing onto a nearby chair? or C) Sit on the edge of the bed and try to slither out of all your clothes in one movement, leaving them to implode into a messy heap on the floor while you whip beneath the sheet?

Or do you ignore your clothing all together and turn to your companion, beginning to undress her/him in the middle of the room, a passionate kiss here, a delicate caress there . . . all the time praying she/he understands that this is a two-way endeavor. Otherwise in a few moments you stand facing a nude partner while you are still in full armor, as it were, and are once again faced with A, B or C.

Of course it all works out in the end. Clothes are somehow shed, lights are turned off or remain on, covers are left on or kicked aside and pillows accept heads. Noses stop bumping and teeth stop clicking. What at first seemed like at least a dozen arms and shoulders sort themselves out and revert to the original number. Legs entwine or loosen at agreeable times, and concave accommodates convex as if architecturally designed.

Then it becomes wondrous indeed to contemplate how two bodies can at the same time be so pleasured and so pleasuring. At least, that's how it worked for Janet and me.

Now we sat at my kitchen table, enjoying that *après*-sex kind of lazy high. She had on my terry cloth robe. I had thrown on a sweatshirt and pair of khakis. We were drinking coffee and munching on two rather stale doughnuts, which were all my larder seemed to offer except for a can of chili, some frozen dinners, a head of wilted lettuce, a saucer of finely aged lasagna, a little carton of what might once have been Chinese take-out and some saltines of uncertain vintage.

"I'm sorry about the doughnuts," I smiled. "Don't break a tooth."

"They're fine," she smiled back. "And I'm not really hungry anyway. Lunch—and everything—was so wonderful." She smiled again, but it looked sad to me.

"Are you okay? You seem . . . forlorn."

"I'm fine!" She straightened in the chair and assumed a cheerful aspect. "I'm just crazy, I guess, but sometimes when everything is just about perfect, and I know I should be happy, I feel sad because I'm afraid things will all go wrong and it will end badly. Do you ever feel that way?"

55

"I don't think so. If you start feeling that way, then no matter how great the moment is, you'll be remembering that someday you'll get old, or sick or fall off a cliff and die! Of course, logically, I know this will happen to me at some point, but I'd just as soon not put a damper on the moment, if you don't mind."

She laughed. "No wonder I like you, you're so openly pragmatic! Oh, I'm very practical about things, but I have a ridiculously hard time with feelings. You seem to have some sort of balance between being sensitive and sensible. I seem to set myself up for disappointment and then fall apart when it happens. I wonder why I'm like that? I always have been."

"Maybe you count too much on other people and not enough on yourself." I thought for a minute. "I'm not sure how to put this. Nobody's perfect. At some point your lover, your boss, your friend—hell—your mother is going to let you down. Maybe they're ill or tired or busy or upset themselves about something. All of a sudden you need their help or their consolation or advice and they give you a blank look. You have to move quickly to Plan B, which is counting on yourself. Sure, it's a disappointment. But it's not the end of the world, nor even necessarily the end of the relationship with the other person. I try to be there for certain people—folks I care about, or people I've made a professional commitment to, but I know there are times I've failed. It doesn't mean I don't care or won't be there next time. It's life," I finished grandly.

Janet's mouth took on a stubborn line. "I cannot imagine letting down someone I care for. No matter what the personal cost to me. If you care for someone, you owe them your best, every time."

"You're a better man than I am, Gunga Din." I kept it light, but I sensed that somewhere, sometime, someone had let Janet down . . . and badly.

"Not really. I have the feeling that you're strong and reliable and one of those terribly honorable types."

"Yeah, well, it's a 'thin red line of 'eroes when the drums begin to roll.'" She was embarrassing me and I was being silly to cover it.

"You're the one who's red," she teased. "Don't you like compliments?"

"Depends what you're complimenting." I gave her a grinning leer.

"Oh, okay, I could hand out a few on that subject, too."

"A few! A few! Talk about letting people down!"

"Talk about conceit!"

We laughed and chatted on, and Janet remarked how relaxed she felt. Truth to tell, I was getting a little nervous. The clock seemed to be speeding, and soon I would need to do the same if I were to complete my assignment regarding Ray Miller. Then, to delay things further, Sonny arrived.

I could have wished he'd picked another time. I liked to keep my personal life personal, although I don't suppose it really mattered. Sonny and I never commented on each other's choice of partners or sexual activities. It was probably the one area in our lives that was off limits to the other, for the simple reason it would probably have led to bloodshed otherwise.

Janet was obviously embarrassed and excused herself to get dressed. Unfazed, Sonny helped himself to a beer from the fridge and took her place at the table, pushing away the stale doughnut scraps with a look of distaste. "Going to the store soon, Alex? These would poison a seagull and your refrigerator looks like a high school chemistry project."

"I'm so glad you stopped by, Sonny. Want to borrow my white gloves and run your finger around the baseboard while you're here?"

"No thanks. I'm allergic to dust and mold. I just came by to tell you what a truly superior detective your brother really is."

"Oh?"

"Yeah. Jake Maxwell was flying his Cessna back from a trip to Boston. He spotted something bright yellow adrift in the water and radioed the Coast Guard. Guess what it turned out to be? An empty Zodiac!"

I saw Janet start across the living room and then hesitate, as if not certain she should join us. "Come on in," I called. "I don't think this is top secret." I turned back to Sonny. "Well, doesn't that pretty much bear out the Plymouth police theory that the robbers couldn't handle it in the storm, went overboard from the big boat or fell out of the Zodiac and drowned?"

"Maybe. But once again there are those little discrepancies. The gas tank of the Zodiac was bone dry. Of course, they could have got the motor running and then fell out, so it just ran around until it ran out of gas. But, Mr. Watson, the tiller was lashed so the Zodiac would run straight."

"I don't get it," Janet interjected. "What does that mean?"

"I'll tell you what I think it means," Sonny replied. "I think they got it going just fine. I think they came ashore in Provincetown. And unless there was some really far-out, unimaginably complex conspiracy and somebody was here to meet them with a car, I think they're right here. They could have come ashore, lashed the tiller in place and sent the Zodiac back out into the bay empty, hoping it would get carried out to sea by the time it ran out of gas, and never be found."

"Yes," I added, "Or they may have hoped if someone did find it, they would know what those things cost and keep it for themselves, rather than reporting the find. But, Sonny, we're forgetting . . ." I glanced at Janet. "You know, the foot. Whoever the man was, he was badly injured, and he'd been in freezing water and then in the cold air. He'd have had to get immediate medical attention or die! I mean, you couldn't have just bandaged up the leg and somehow got him into a motel or something."

"I know. Actually, when I was saying 'they,' I should have said 'he.' I think the big guy went overboard and got hurt and probably drowned fairly early on. Even if the little man somehow got him into the Zodiac, I imagine he died soon. Loss of blood, shock." Sonny glanced at Janet. She was leaning against the sink, a little pale but seemingly not about to faint. "Then," he continued, "I think the smaller guy dumped him or left him or whatever and came ashore. If either of you see a little Hispanic guy wandering around, you call me."

"It makes sense," I admitted. "He doesn't know the Bertram's boat cushions and the Zodiac were found. Presumably he has money. He could rent a room and just figure he'll lie low until things calm down and then quietly leave. He probably has money from the Plymouth robberies."

I thought of all the talk in the Wharf Rat. "Sonny, if so many people think this is drug-related, couldn't they be right? I mean, these robbers—couldn't they have been hitting all those Plymouth stores to get cash for drugs? And couldn't they really have planned to make some sort of pick-up at sea and just got caught in the storm?"

"Yeah, that could be the story," Sonny nodded. "And there are always crazy things happening with drug buys . Not enough cash, bad product, personal quarrels, and—in this case—maybe just plain bad weather."

I lit a cigarette, and Sonny took it from me as he continued. "My main problem is the Zodiac and the little man. Anyway, we're going to start checking around any motels and B&Bs that are open this time of year. Now don't get macho and approach this guy if you see him, Alex. He may still have a gun, and he sure in hell has nothing to lose. I, on the other hand, would just as soon not lose my sister. At least not permanently."

"There speaks the big brother," Janet smiled fondly.

"Um, very sweet," I muttered, somehow embarrassed that Sonny would vocalize affection. "Okay. If I see this guy, I'll run for the cell phone."

"That's an excellent—not to say sensible—idea," Janet agreed. "But there's another thought that keeps going through my mind. What did you say was the name of the people in Plymouth who kept falling down the steps? McKinley?"

"McKinney, I think." Sonny grinned in remembrance.

"Okay. Either way, it's Irish and a lot of the Irish in the Boston area are IRA supporters. They're not all barflies who think they've done a great thing if they toss a fiver into the hat at the pub, you know, there's some big money involved, too. The McKinneys could have supplied the boat and paid for the two men to run illegal firearms out to some ship. And something went wrong. A fight, an accident, murder."

I found myself beaming at Janet's idea. It was both creative and logical! Didn't we make a fine pair? Maybe we could combine our analytical talents. Peres and Meacham, Private Investigators. Oops, she didn't know that about me yet. Well, soon.

Sonny sighed deeply. "Lord, Janet, you're beginning to sound like Alex. Next you'll being trying to tell me they went out to meet a ship carrying illegal Chinese immigrants!"

Janet laughed. "How about South American or Caribbean instead? They'd be less obvious than fifty new Chinese suddenly wandering around the town."

"Come on, Sonny," I pursued. "It could be drugs or it could be IRA. You just want it to be your robbers. Don't be so stubborn. There's a difference between being focused and having tunnel vision, you know."

"Oh, hell, all right. But I will not call the FBI. If I do we'll have ten of 'em running around looking under every clam shell. I will ask the Plymouth police to take a quiet look at the McKinneys. I know Bob Reynolds pretty well over there. And I will call Chief Wood at the Coast Guard Station—unofficially. He's a wise old bird. Okay? Enough? Will you two promise not to have any more bright ideas?"

"I suppose so, detective," I smiled sweetly. "Although I would think the police would be grateful for assistance from concerned citizens."

"Alex! You can be the most irritating . . ."

Janet interrupted him by standing up noisily. "I'm going to run for the hills, commonly known as Mrs. Madeiros' place," Janet said. "I've really got to get back."

"Don't let me interrupt your evening," said Sonny. "I have to go home. I promised Mom I'd be there for dinner."

"You're not interrupting. I'm a little tired." She blushed prettily. "And I want to get up early in the morning to get some writing done. That's my best time."

"Well, if you're sure. Are you walking? Can I give you a ride?" She thanked him and nodded.

With surprising tact, Sonny took Fargo out into the back yard, giving Janet and me time to say our good-byes. We kissed gently, concurred that the day had been great and agreed that Janet would call me the next morning.

As they drove away, I looked at my watch and swore. I was running late if Ray was on schedule. I grabbed my coat and called the dog. I decided not to go by Miller's house and hope he would still be there, but to go directly to Marcia Robby's, hoping that Sonny was correct in saying Miller went there on Thursdays. This way I would have time to swing by the drive-in over on Bradford and pick up something to eat. Maybe Janet could live on doughnut crumbs. I was starved.

I dashed into the restaurant and ordered a cheeseburger with the works and a large fries for myself, a plain burger for Fargo, a Diet Coke for now and coffee for later. Three minutes and I was rolling back toward Marcia's. She lived almost to the end of Commercial Street in the West End. The bottom floor of the house was her Select Antiques store, which included anything not ostensibly new.

She lived upstairs. I'd been in her apartment a time or two, and it was charming—as light and airy and uncluttered as her store was dim and crowded and fusty with the aroma of lemon oil.

The clutter served to showcase Marcia's dramatic talents. When prospective buyers came in she would ask them to describe their home a little, so she could visualize them in it and "feel what they felt it called out for." Then she would walk directly past various pieces to, say, a table. She would stroke it lightly. "This. I can feel this would find the perfect spot in your home. But it is expensive and you have told me you are on a budget and I understand that. So . . . !"

And she would leave it and walk to other tables in the shop, always glancing back at the first with a warm smile and soft eyes, but resolutely telling the virtues of some other, cheaper tables. Suddenly, she would turn away, pressing her fingers to her eyes. "No. No. I cannot sell this cheaper piece to you. You can afford it. I would make some small profit, but later you would never forgive me. I cannot let you take what isn't right for you. In the long run you will think more highly of me if you take nothing. I am sorry, perhaps you should simply go."

Nine times out of ten she had a check or credit card for the more expensive piece in less than five minutes.

I admired her acting ability and salesmanship, but one small part of me believed she really meant all she said. Several years ago she and Sonny had a brief liaison right after his first wife had left him, taking his small son with her. He hadn't cared so much about his wife, but he was truly heartbroken over losing a lot of his contact with the little boy.

During that period I ran into Marcia at the Wharf Rat and we had a drink together. I happened to mention I had that afternoon found a sandpiper with a broken leg and taken it to my vet to be patched up.

She put her hand on mine for a moment and smiled. "Perhaps we both do a service in this town, Alex. You care for the flying wounded and I for the walking wounded." At the time I thought it was the martini talking, but later I realized what she had meant. And now I was spying on her. Sometimes I really loved my job.

I parked a couple of houses before Marcia's, and Fargo and I wolfed down our dinners with about the same amount of grace. I saw headlights coming up behind me and slid down below window level until they passed. He parked right in front of the shop. I got a couple of shots of him ringing her bell and one of her letting him in. With my latest camera the prints would be automatically date and time stamped. I settled down to wait, figuring I might as well wrap the whole thing up with a photo of him saying a perhaps passionate goodnight. I just hoped it wouldn't be the middle of the night.

Tempus didn't fugit. I was having an awful time staying awake. No matter what I tried thinking about, it started to put me to sleep. Thoughts about neither sex nor murder could seem to hold my interest. I was tired, and right this moment one seemed as dull as the other. I finished the Diet Coke and started on the lukewarm coffee. Next I'd probably have to pee. What a way to end a great day. All I needed was some neighbor to walk out his door as I stumbled bleary eyed from his shrubbery, pulling up my pants.

Finally, *finally*, lights went on downstairs. The door opened and Miller came out. He did not embrace her. He actually sort of bowed and kissed her hand. I wondered how far this would go with a divorce lawyer. But then, I doubted if Diane Miller had any thoughts of divorce. I felt she wanted information just to shorten Ray's leash, and this would probably be enough to put Ray right smack in the doghouse exactly where she wanted him. I really didn't care. I didn't even bother to follow Ray home. If he stopped somewhere for a drink, I cared not. I was just very grateful the evening was over and I could go to my nice warm bed.

Fargo did his evening chores while I quickly brushed my teeth and donned my pajamas. He jumped into bed beside me, sniffed the pillows and immediately began to make that whuffling noise dogs make, like they are blowing air out through their lips. The vet says it simply means they are processing an unfamiliar scent, but somehow it always sounds disapproving to me.

"Fargo! Settle down or get down!"

He stopped whuffling and lay down. Then he rearranged himself several times, managing to give me a couple of mule-kicks in the middle of my back as he did so. I chose to assume they were accidental.

"Dammit, Fargo!" He sighed deeply and lay still. I burrowed into the pillow, still faintly reminiscent of Janet's cologne, and may have whuffled a bit myself. But almost immediately I began to drift into sleep.

As I did so, I began a beautiful, colorful dream. I was steering a deep purple Bertram cabin cruiser through a lovely, calm lavender sea. Janet stood smiling beside me, both of us clad in woad-colored sailor uniforms. She pointed to the rear of the boat. There, bobbing merrily along behind us on a short tow rope, was a giant, bright yellow sneaker.

"What is it?" I asked stupidly.

"It's a Zodiac."

"It looks like a sneaker."

"You silly goose. Surely I know a Zodiac when I see one. I was an admiral in the Coast Guard. And look here."

She waved a large piece of stiff, heavy pink paper in front of my face. At the top was a graceful pen and ink sketch of a smiling Janet in a toga, reclining on a Roman couch, holding a bunch of magenta grapes over a glass of pale yellow wine. Printed beneath the sketch in large ornate gold calligraphy were the words "Filet of Sole *Veronique*."

"It's the menu to my famous new restaurant, and sole *Veronique* and your Aunt Mae's borage herb bread are all I'm going to serve." She hugged me and smiled. "But don't worry. I'll always make scallops and french fries for *you*."

Thus reassured, I sighed and fell more deeply asleep.

# Chapter 7

I slept well and was awakened early Friday morning by a breathy and cavernous yawn in my right ear.

"Good morning, Fargo."

He stood with his front paws on the pillow and grinned down at me, teeth bared, looking totally ferocious. Then he flopped onto his back for a belly scratch, with all four legs in the air, looking totally ludicrous. I let him outdoors while I showered and made a pot of coffee. I let him in and gave him fresh water and food. Finally, I settled at the kitchen table, feeling totally indolent and quite content with my world. Fargo let me enjoy my lazy morning until after my second leisurely cup of coffee. Then he started a series of tentative tail wags and elbow nudges and deep sighs. Reluctantly, I let myself be cajoled into a trip to Race Point.

Well, obviously I had to go sometime. And sooner was probably better than later, before I let my reluctance to visit the scene of the unpleasant discovery build into something more important than it really was. I took my camera with the black and white film along, telling myself it was just another working day to build up my collection of photos for the summer season.

It was a calm and somewhat dank morning, with a low fog bank lying sullenly just offshore. It did not dull Fargo's pleasure, although I shivered in the chill as he ran along splashing noisily and happily in the cold wavelets, hoping as always for gulls to torment or sandpipers to herd along the shallows.

As we walked along, I noticed an interestingly shaped piece of driftwood lying half-buried in the sand. Near it was an old wooden lobster-pot marker with worn-away paint, and a few feet further on, the carapace of a long-dead crab. I resolutely refused to think of errant feet as I arranged them artistically and took a couple of close-ups from different angles. Look, 'nature' photos are not always exactly 'natural,' okay?

After I figured Fargo had had enough exercise for the morning, I picked up the driftwood and marker, and took them along as we walked back to the car. I would give them both to Aunt Mae. Come the summer, she'd place them attractively among her herb displays and someone would give her a good price for them. Tourists. Never forget the tourists—or their wallets.

On the way back to town I remembered I'd better stop by the bank for some cash. Fortunately, the ATM was actually working, and there was no line this early in the day, so my visit was blessedly brief, and we were on our way home again when I noticed a young man walking up Commercial Street. He was slight and of dark complexion, which was not at all unusual in Provincetown, but I didn't recognize him and he seemed somehow uneasy in his gait. He wasn't exactly looking over his shoulder, but he impressed me as being wary of his surroundings. I slowed the car and finally stopped and saw him turn down the alley toward the Wharf Rat Bar.

Joe's wife Billie usually opened the bar in the mornings and did the cleaning, such as it was, and handled any early business, such as it was. She was also the lunch cook, and not a bad one, either. Joe didn't come in to tend bar and serve food until around eleven, when the traffic began to pick up. My curiosity was piqued. Not too many people visit bars at 9:15 in the morning, even in Provincetown, and most of them are the regular daylong drinkers you find ensconced in every bar from the moment the key turns in the lock. I had never seen this kid around the Rat at any time, and from a distance he didn't look old enough to drink, whatever the hour. Of course, he could be job hunting or looking for someone, or maybe he was a lot older than he looked. And of course, there was one good way to find out.

I parked the car and rolled the windows down for Fargo and gave him a drink and a biscuit from his stash in the back seat. As I walked down the alley, I saw that Billie had the door propped open to let the morning light in and the night's smoke and beer and booze smell out—or as out as it ever got. I stood in the doorway for a moment, letting my eyes adjust. Even on a dull morning the interior of the Wharf Rat was considerably dimmer than the outdoors. Then I strolled in, barely missing a pail full of grey water and a mop precariously standing in it.

One regular was already settled in at the end of the bar with a draft beer. It was Sergeant York. At least that was what everyone called him. If I ever knew his real name, I can't remember it. He had been a Marine hero in WWII in the Pacific, and he regaled anyone who would even pretend to listen to him with detailed battle histories by the hour. If no one were handy, he'd talk to himself, as he was doing now. Around noon he'd move on to Kelly's Bar and Grill, later he'd call in at the Fisherman's Bar and finally back to the Rat, where around ten in the evening, someone would drive him home.

I looked at the level in his glass of beer. It wasn't that he drank so much. Actually he didn't. He simply had no place to go. He shared his house with a yuppie son, a snippy daughter-in-law and a squeaky clean little snob of a granddaughter. The house was impersonally furnished according to Better Homes, pages seventeen through twenty, and kept ready for invasion by the Ladies' Aid Society at any time. It had no comfortable place for an old man who hourly relived the triumphs of his young life and spilled mustard on his shirt.

"Morning, Sergeant! It's a fine day for March. Not too cold and not too hot but just right, as they say."

"Good morning, Miss. A bit foggy though. Good enemy weather, we would have said on the Canal."

"Yessir. A day to exercise caution, I'm sure." I moved on down the bar to where the young man sat with an impressive stack of money in front of him. Billie leaned across the bar toward him with a look of irritation on her face, tempered by little greedy glances at the pile of bills on the bar.

"Hi, Billie. What's up?"

"I'm up, that's what, and way too early on a damp day like this, if you ask me, which you did. And this young pup is sittin' here demanding a Mudslide cocktail, which sounds like we oughta be in California which we certainly aren't, as I don't have any idea how to make even if he would show me some ID so's I knew if I should even try and look it up if he did."

"Right." It paid to listen closely when Billie spoke. I turned to the young man. "Why won't you show the lady some ID, so she can look up how she might make your drink, if you have any, that is?" I grimaced. Was Billie's syntax contagious?

"None of your business." His dark eyes flashed under the brim of his cap, and the wispy wannabe mustache quivered with indignation. Obviously he intended to brazen out this scene. Two mere women weren't going to keep him from his Mudslide.

"Where'd you get all that money?"

"Who the hell do you think you are? Somebody die and make you chief of the curious police?"

Silently, I pulled the laminated copy of my Private Investigator's license out of my pocket, expertly covered the word 'Private' with my thumb and let the word "Investigator" and the gaudy Great Seal of Massachusetts work their silent magic.

He grabbed for his money and ran for the door, but I was ready for that. I simply stuck out my foot and tripped him, watched him lose his footing on the wet, freshly mopped floor and fall face down onto the damp boards. I put my foot casually on the back of his neck. When he struggled, I increased the pressure on his neck till he quit and lay quiet, and then I stood there looking down at him with an expression of extreme distaste.

"Well done! Well done!" Sergeant York applauded.

"Thank you, sir. Billie, would you please call the police station and ask my brother to come over if he's there. If he's not, anyone who's free will do." I remembered belatedly that my cell phone was in the car and that I had promised not to confront any Hispanic-looking strangers, so I rather hoped that Sonny might *not* be available right this moment.

I'm all too aware that crime is not age-specific anymore, but I had a hard time thinking this slightly built infant was armed and dangerous. But I also knew that could be a good way to get killed, so I checked his pockets and legs as best I could. He was apparently unarmed, so I removed most of the pressure from his neck.

What disturbed me was the money. It was scattered around him, all twenties it seemed, and looked like several hundred dollars. I tried again. "I will ask you once again, where'd you get the money? I want to know, and right now, Fast Track."

"Fuck you, dyke."

I kicked him gently in the head. Hey, I was wearing sneakers! "Mind your manners or I'll pour this pail of mop water down your throat and you'll die clutching your belly and moaning in agony. One more time, slime mouth. Where did you get all that money?"

"I earned it," he muttered sullenly. "It's mine."

At that moment a police car screamed to a halt in the alley, no more than a foot from the door. Officer Mitchell strode in, pistol at the ready in his hand. I wondered briefly what on earth Billie must have said on the phone. He looked at the money spread around the floor and then at Billie. "What did he do, try to rob the place?"

Before she could answer, he turned to me. "Alex, are you okay?"

"She's just fine, patrolman, she has landed and got the situation well in hand!" Sergeant York was gleeful.

I managed to get a word in for myself. "I'm okay, Mitch. No harm done. This fine specimen was trying to buy a drink with no ID and a lot of unexplained money he says is his." I picked the bills up off the floor as Mitch holstered his 9mm Glock. "If he has any ID he's not showing it, and he won't say who he is or where he got this. Looks like he's got about two hundred dollars here."

I handed it to Mitch, who counted it and buttoned it into his jacket pocket. "I make it one-eighty."

I asked him, "Did Sonny happen to mention to you that he was on the lookout for a slim, dark complected young man, maybe with a mustache? Somebody new in town, a stranger?"

"Yeah, he told us. Sonny's in court this morning. But I never saw your fine specimen around town before. I'll take him in and let Sonny talk to him later. He said he hoped to be back before noon. Come on, macho man, get up and put your hands behind your back." The boy got reluctantly to his feet, and Mitch reached for his cuffs. As he started to handcuff the young man, we both noticed marks on the boy's wrists. "What's this," Mitch asked, "You *already* been cuffed this morning? You're a busy man."

"It's just a rash," the boy muttered.

"Some rash! Looks like rope burns to me," Mitch said. "I don't want to cuff him, Alex. I could make his 'rash' worse and then he'd have a nice brutality complaint to file, which he'd love to do if I know his type. And regulations say I can't be in the car alone with him if he isn't cuffed. So now what do I do with him?"

The boy smiled sourly. "Damn right."

"Put him in the car and I'll ride down with you and walk back . . . oh, hell, I can't. My dog's with me."

"My dog's with me," the kid mimicked. "You guys are such fuck-ups. Just let me go and I won't sue you for almost breaking my neck."

At that point I was quite ready to finish the job on his neck and might have fully lost my temper, when I heard a quiet 'ahem' and sensed someone standing behind me.

Sergeant York had walked over to us. "Let me ride along with the officer," he suggested. "I'll just sit in back with the boy. He won't try to go anywhere with me in there with him."

"That's a great idea!" I nodded vigorously to cut off the 'no' I saw forming on Mitch's lips. "Thank you, Sergeant, that's the answer to our problem."

The kid groaned. "Jeez, what kind of crazy town is this? First I get Babble Betty, then the Ditzy Dyke, then Officer Dimwit, now I got Grandad! Oh, dearie me, I'm just fucking-A scared to death!"

Mitch, Billie and I watched in smiling, silent admiration as the kid flew through the air from Sergeant York's upper-cut to the chin. This time he landed on his back on the wet floor and looked up, winded, to find the old man standing over him, large booted foot resting lightly on his crotch. "Now, son, you got to quit usin' those words in front of ladies! You just take it real easy there, and I'll help you up." York bent over and offered his enormous hand. The boy took it, and the next thing I knew, he was on his feet, turned around, his arm bent up somewhere near his shoulder blade and being frog-marched to the police car.

"Well, Mitch, I don't think you'll have any trouble between here and the station," I couldn't help but chuckle.

"I have a feeling we'll manage."

"Um. Say, Mitch, ask the old guy to stay for your coffee-and-doughnuts break. You know, make him feel important, like he's really done something helpful."

He stared at me for a moment, and then he understood and nodded seriously. "Yes. Good idea. My Dad says the Sergeant was quite a man in his time. And I'll make sure word gets around to his family how much he 'assisted us in our inquiries', too." I like Mitch. Sometimes I think there's hope for men.

I turned back to Billie who was standing in the doorway. "Sorry for the commotion," I apologized.

"Oh, no harm done." She gave a raspy laugh. "Kinda did my

71

heart good. Snotty kid like that and first he gets knocked down by a woman and then by an old man, like you'd think he'd learn, but you want to bet he won't, as that type rarely does profit from a lesson until it's too late nowadays if they do."

"Right! Well, see you, Billie."

I got to the car feeling pure of heart, and this time we made it home.

It was nearly ten and I wondered if Janet had called. The answer machine wasn't blinking, so I figured she was sleeping in or deep into composing the next best seller. I heated up a cup of coffee in the microwave and went into the office to gather the photos of Ray Miller into chronological order and write up a report and a bill for his wife, Diane. I'd be glad to wrap it up. I felt half sorry for and half irritated with everyone involved.

As I waited for the computer to boot up, I thought about Marcia Robby and wondered what she saw in Ray. She was French-Canadian, and although her English was idiomatic and accent-free, somehow you knew it was not her first language. She was undoubtedly pushing fifty. Her black curly mane was beginning to grey, but her figure was good, her features clean-cut. Some of the Ptown biddies dubbed her a scarlet woman, but she really wasn't. Some of the men who'd never spent five minutes alone with her called her an easy lay. She wasn't, sensual aura not withstanding.

I had a feeling she dispensed more tea and sympathy than sex. And though I knew she wasn't averse to a fling with a good-looking guy, she obviously had no desire for permanence. I knew of several men who'd have happily married her, but she'd have none of them. I'd heard her mention a long-gone husband once or twice, but always accompanied by a little flick of the fingers, as if annoyed by something sticky and not quite nice.

Bottom line: I liked her and hoped Diane Miller wouldn't cause her any discomfort or embarrassment. I'd have to try and make sure we avoided that, somehow.

As I finished pecking out my report, I figured I had been right about Diane. I still thought she was less interested in leaving Ray than in accumulating some relatively genteel blackmail as insurance to keep *him* from leaving *her*. At that moment Fargo ran to the door with a kind of half-bark, as if he weren't quite sure what he was supposed to do. There was a 'shave-and-a-haircut' knock on the door, which indicated that Sonny had arrived.

"Come on in," I yelled. "I'm in the office."

But, surprisingly, it was Janet who entered, and I jumped up to give her an enthusiastic kiss. Fargo seemed more interested in a bag she held at her side. "Pastries," she said, as she lifted it away from his nose. "I thought breakfast might be in order. And I thought those doughnuts from yesterday would qualify as antiques by this morning." She smiled impishly.

"Replacements are long overdue!" I kissed her again with the fleeting hope that my nose wasn't suddenly wet and quivering in concert with Fargo's. "Let's make some fresh coffee and eat."

"What's all this?" Janet had noticed the photographs of Ray Miller spread across the table and was now staring at the computer.

"Damn! I shouldn't have left all this stuff out. It's supposed to be confidential. I would have put it away, but I thought you were going to give me a call before you came over."

"I was," she said. "I went up to the corner to the pay phone—I've really got to get a phone in my apartment, don't I?—but someone was gabbing away, so I just started walking to find another phone. Then I stopped and picked up the pastry, and by then I was halfway here, so I just came along. But what is all this? What do you mean it's confidential? I thought you were a nature photographer."

She caught herself up short. "I'm sorry. I didn't mean to pry. It just surprised me. Forget I said that . . . it's not my business. I'm sorry I didn't call. I didn't know it would matter." She turned away, flustered.

"It's not your fault at all. It's mine." As I rattled on, flustered myself, I hurriedly shoved the photos and report into my briefcase. "I guess it's confession time. I do take a lot of nature photos and sell

73

them, but that's not my primary livelihood by a long shot. Actually, I'm a P.I.—a private investigator. You see, I don't usually tell people right off because sometimes they think it's some kind of joke or else they seem to feel somewhat . . ."

I realized I was talking to myself. Janet had walked on into the kitchen and was sitting at the table with her head in her hands, laughing almost hysterically, as if she'd never stop.

I was angry, hurt, surprised. I hadn't expected this reaction from her. Somehow I had just assumed she would understand. "I don't see what's so goddam funny," I said harshly. "It's a perfectly legitimate job." I pulled her hands away from her face and glared down at her. "God knows it's no flakier than deciding to write a novel just because you broke up with somebody and have nothing else to do, or having some damn fool restaurant where you only serve Sole *Veronique* or scallops!" In my anger I didn't realize I was mixing fact with last night's dream.

Cheeks still wet with tears, she looked up at me with a rueful grin.

"What the hell have I gotten myself into? Your brother is a cop. You're a P.I. What's your mother, the district attorney?"

# Chapter 8

Well, I had to admit, she had a point there. My anger quickly faded and I couldn't help grinning back at her, as I answered, "No my mother's not the DA. In fact, you might say she works the other side of the street. She's just a nice protestant lady who works part time in the office at the local Catholic Church."

"I don't care. It's still law enforcement." Janet's smile turned grumpy. "The cop tells you what you can't do. If you do it anyway, you are punished. What's the difference in him and a priest?"

"I guess it is somewhat the same, maybe a little more gently phrased . . . or sometimes maybe not." I laughed, and that earned me a quavery smile. "Hey, I'm sorry if I jumped all over you. It's just that I'm kind of sensitive on the subject of my profession, I guess. It doesn't have to be pure sleaze and peering into bedroom windows, you know. In fact, most of being a P.I. is kind of interesting—at least I think so."

I ticked off items on my fingers. "Some fraud, or tracking down missing relatives or people named in a will, investigating potential employees, finding runaway kids. It's by no means confined to following errant spouses around town. But add my touch of paranoia to the really crazy morning I've already had, and maybe you'll forgive me for being just a tad prickly today."

We settled down with fresh coffee and the big cranberry-walnut scones. They tasted wonderful. As we ate, I told her of my earlier adventures.

"Do you think this kid could be part of that robber gang?" Janet was dubious. "He wanted to get away badly enough, but he doesn't quite seem to fit the picture."

"It's hard to believe he's old enough or savvy enough, but he's obviously no boy scout. Tough little bastard and street-smart. I don't know. He's awfully young, but that doesn't mean much anymore."

"I know. It's awful. I heard on the news this morning about a thirteen-year-old-boy who murdered a little six-year-old-girl for not forking over her lunch money. It's scary, isn't it? Whoever thought you'd have to be afraid of grammar-school kids? But anyway, back to the beginning. Do I dare ask how you ever ended up as a private investigator in a small town like this? Somehow you think of private investigators as being in Boston or New York."

"It's simple enough," I told her. "I wanted to be a lawyer when I was a kid, but my father's untimely demise put an end to that possibility." I told her of my father's death, and she reacted with predictable horror. I continued with my tale.

"Well, it sure put the kibosh on four years of college plus law school. We were actually in pretty dire straits for a few years there. I don't really know how Mom held it together as well as she did. I did manage to get a student loan and get to the community college up in Hyannis. I lived at home and that helped."

Janet broke a scone in half and put it on her plate. I got up and poured us more coffee, and then snagged the half-pastry she had left on the platter.

"I suppose if I had been truly dedicated, I could have gotten a job in Boston and lived in some dreary little room and gone to night school. But truth to tell, I just didn't have that kind of ambition. I didn't want to be a poverty-ridden drudge in a big city for ten years until I could get my law degree. I didn't want to be starting my legal career when most of my peer group would be already well established at some good firm. I'm where I want to be. A large percentage of the time I enjoy what I'm doing. Financially I'm really pretty much okay."

I reached down and rubbed a silky ear. "And here in Ptown I can have Fargo and take him most anywhere I go. So, I guess the bottom line is—no regrets."

Janet cocked her head. "Really no regrets? Don't you feel that your father and mother pretty much let you down?"

"Let me down? I really doubt that my father, for all his myriad faults, picked up a ten-thousand-volt electric line just so he wouldn't feel he had to help me with my college tuition!" I heard my voice rise and made an effort to calm down.

"For several years Mom was hard-put to hang onto the house and get us through high school. And for my two years in Community she wouldn't take a cent of rent or board. She helped me out with every dollar she could. That's what really made it possible for me. No, Janet, I'd hardly call that letting me down!"

"Well, if you say so." She didn't sound terribly convinced. "I didn't get to college at all, and it was no more my fault than it was yours. I was really counting on my high school advisor to help me get a scholarship, hopefully to Cornell. I wanted desperately to major in cooking and restaurant management and a Cornell degree gets you an immediate entree most anywhere in that field. My high school grades were quite good and I had a part-time job at Burger King, not that it was any great restaurant, of course, but it showed interest and willingness to work hard. But strangely, it turned out that kids with lower grades and any old kind of job at all got the scholarships."

Her voice was bitter and harsh. I couldn't understand what she was getting at. "So, no Cornell? What happened?"

"No Cornell." Janet nodded. "Strangely, my high school counselor seems to have successfully blocked that. On the surface it appeared that she tried very hard for me. Her recommendations were all glowing with statements like 'she is deeply dedicated . . . ' or 'she works every spare moment . . . ' or 'she lets nothing stand in the way of . . . ' or 'she will make painful sacrifices to obtain . . . ' She made me sound like some sort of fixated lunatic."

I didn't understand. "Why would she do that?"

"She may have been incompetent or may have just disliked me. But I heard she was one of those radical evangelical people. Maybe she found out I was a lesbian and made sure there'd be no scholarships for this sinful kid. In any event, there were none."

We looked at each other and shrugged. Homophobia could be a bitch. "So you joined the Coasties?"

She stuck her tongue out at me for using the nickname but grinned her forgiveness. "Well, not immediately. I still had hopes of getting into some college. I started trying to get student loans for colleges that were within commuting distance. I figured if I could live at home for nothing, and work part time, with a loan I could probably swing it."

"Not too many colleges you can very easily commute to around New Hampshire," I mused. "You can't have had many choices. Could you have found one that offered the major you wanted?"

Janet looked down at the table, her hands clasped hard around her coffee mug. She spoke, so softly I had trouble hearing her. I leaned forward as she said, "Alex, I'm not from New Hampshire, and my folks aren't comfortably retired and living happily down in Florida. I'm from Connecticut, and my folks live right where they always have—in a shabby old two-family house in a blue-collar section of Norwalk. I—I lied. I was ashamed of my background. I wanted you to think I came from a regular middle class family, not a bunch of lowbrows who think Emily Dickinson is Angie's sister."

I laughed, but then sobered when I realized how much all this obviously meant to her. I asked, "Surely you don't think I'm an heiress in disguise? Or that I give a damn about your family? It's you I care about," I said, and suddenly realized that I did indeed care.

"No, I don't think you are an heiress." She managed a weak smile. "But I don't think your family is like mine, either. Not by a long shot. And maybe you don't care about my family, but I do. They're pretty awful. Their idea of a gala evening is to spend every Saturday night at the VFW club, where they drink too much and come home either antagonistic or amorous. I don't know which is worse."

My father would have fit right in, I mused. His drinking got to a point where Mom would rarely even go out socially with him. And when she did, she usually came home silent and tight-lipped. And we all tiptoed around his next day's hangover. I knew right where Janet was. I knew how that problem could affect a family.

She ran her hand nervously through her short curls. "I'm the youngest of five—an older sister and three older brothers. I watched them grow up and only one of them finished high school. Except for my brother Eddie, they're all like junior editions of my mother and father. They have dead-end jobs and sit on the front porch and drink beer and sweat and burp. The men talk about the Yankees or the Jets, and the women argue over whether Pathmark or Grand Union has cheaper canned goods. From the time I was little, I swore that no matter *what* I had to do, *wherever* I had to go . . . I would be different!"

"And you are," I smiled reassuringly. "You're intelligent and ambitious and well-mannered. Hell," I teased gently, "In a weak moment one might well refer to you as a fine lady. Come on, Janet, you are yourself, not your family. *You* have nothing to be ashamed of."

She gave me a startled, almost haunted look, and laughed strangely. I began to be sorry we'd gotten into this. If her family bothered her that much, I'd just as soon have left them in their fairy tale—cozy and happy and sober and financially comfortable in

Florida via New Hampshire. Who gave a damn? But Janet took a breath and began to speak again, rather hurriedly, as if now that she'd started this dreary saga she must complete it.

"Back in the Middle ages when they switched babies, what did they call it?"

"You mean a changeling?"

"Yes, that's it," she agreed. "When I was a kid I swore I was a changeling, and to this day I'm still not sure the hospital didn't screw up the ID tags. My family was chunky and square—I was slender. My brothers—well, two of them—were lazy and crude. My sister would rather have four cheap, fancy sweaters than one good plain one. If you said the word 'opera' to any of them, they would immediately mentally preface it with 'Grand Old.'" She smiled ruefully. "Anyway, I got my student loan and enrolled in the local community college. I figured that would give me two years to try to work something out with Cornell while I took some basic courses."

Something in her distracted gaze told me that kite hadn't flown, either. "So what went wrong?"

"I was optimistic and excited, when I told Mama about it. We were both so happy . . . until Pop got home that night. He said in no uncertain terms I wouldn't be living free at home, 'sponging' off them and getting some silly degree I didn't need anyway. Once I got out of high school, I'd get a job and pay room and board just like the other kids had. He said he had lots of 'expenses to consider', like God forbid he'd have to give up a few beers at the VFW! My mother didn't say one word to try to change his mind! I was frantic."

"I don't doubt it." This poor kid got shot down at every turn. "What did you do?"

She extended her hands, as if in supplication. "What could I do? I was out of ideas. I felt paralyzed. My only hope was that Pop would give in. About that time my brother Eddie came home on leave. Sergeant Edward Meacham, with his stripes and ribbons and badges . . . oh, I was so proud of him! And I understood before long why he never came home."

She paused while she took one of my cigarettes and lit it. I was surprised and must have looked it. "I don't do this often," she qualified and then continued. "My whole family, including the in-laws and excepting Mama, teased him unmercifully. Did he have to take orders from female officers? Were they dykes or nymphos? What about blacks—only that's not the word they used. Did he have to shower with them? Eat with them? Did he sleep in a barracks with women? On and on."

"What a savory group," I smiled sourly.

"*Weren't* they?" She grimaced back. "One night Eddie took me to dinner. He handed me two-hundred dollars for my graduation and told me to use it to get far, far away from Connecticut and the family before they did me in. 'You're not like them. You're like me,' he said. I liked that. Here was I, borrowing money for school, with Pop telling me I owed him money for board. And here was Eddie, with a great future, happy, with money to spare and a nice girl he planned to marry. That was a surprise."

I was relieved to learn at least one member of her family had some feeling for Janet. Apparently Eddie had given some serious thought to his younger sister's future. Janet filled in more details. "He urged me to join the army, to take advantage of all the opportunities they offered. He gave me his address and said I should keep in touch. He would not be back. He had even told his girl he was an orphan except for me. Oh, I wanted to be like Eddie all right."

"Wow!" I breathed, somewhat taken aback. "That's a pretty definitive farewell to the old plantation, isn't it? So now you joined the Coasties?"

She took a bite from her scone and swallowed. "Yup. I didn't quite see myself firing a cannon or driving a tank." She gave a sort of surprised chuckle. "But you know what? I did get to where I could conn a forty-foot boat in a forty-mile wind and find it exhilarating! It was like a game. At what angle do you approach the next wave to make it easiest on the boat?"

I had a sudden vision of Janet on the wind-blown bridge of a boat, balanced lightly on the balls of her feet, cheeks streaked with water, the wheel grasped firmly in her rather square, capable hands. Oh, to take that photo!

"However," she interrupted my daydream. "My family couldn't even let my enlistment play out pleasantly."

"Let me guess what happened." It wasn't hard. "Your father was against that, too."

"Bingo! My father started stomping around and storming that I wasn't going cavorting around in the service like some cheap hussy, that I would damn well stay home, get a job and help out with things like a normal daughter until I got married."

"But he couldn't stop you—certainly not at that point. When he figured that out, it's probably what made him crazy."

"Well, I'd had enough of him and that time I stormed back, 'Then I'll certainly be a comfort in your old age! I'll never get married—I'm a lesbian!'"

"Brava! Brava!" I cried. "I'll bet that shut them up."

"Far from it," Janet finally laughed and sounded more or less like herself. "Mama started wailing how could I do this to her and Pop was almost frothing at the mouth and came out with one of his typically brilliant remarks. 'Well, if you want to be a queer, don't do it in here!'" She giggled. "He sounded like I was a puppy who was going to pee on the floor or something. So I got my little bag, spent the night with an old school friend and left the next morning."

I washed down the last crumb with a sip of coffee. "That kind of man seems to make people unable to stand up for themselves. My father was a bit like that, although I must admit, not to that degree," I recalled. "Mom always seemed to give into him. I guess it was just easier in the long run than listening to his bluster and criticism and his sort of brooding disapproval."

Janet nodded agreement. "I think you're right. If you're going to live your life with that sort, you pretty much have to do it their way."

"Well," I said, reaching for a cigarette. Number three, only number three! "Mom's very different now, very much her own person. I remember, Sonny always seemed sullen to me as a boy, although he's not at all that way now. And I lived in a kind of pretend world with books and movies where the families were always sweet and happy and baking cookies or making fudge. I hate to say it, but I think all three of us have come off better without Daddy Dearest. Maybe someday your mom will get out from under your father's thumb."

"I don't know. Whenever I've called home, all she does is say how sorry she is. Sometimes she even tries to tell me that deep-down my father loves me, too, in his way."

"But at least you're out. How did it go in the Coast Guard?"

"In the beginning I think it probably saved my life—or at least my sanity. Oh!" Janet jumped as Fargo barked and ran to the back door, tail wagging furiously.

This time it was Sonny. It seemed to me I'd been seeing an awful lot of him lately, which was pleasant enough, but unusual. Actually, his timing could have been a lot better, as I'd been thinking that it might be nice for Janet and me to put all this familial *sturm und drang* behind us with a little meaningful bedroom-time. Now, instead of two for romance, it became three for coffee as Sonny made himself comfortable at the table and reached for a goodie.

"Oh, this is good! This is what you call fresh, Alex. There are stores that actually bake them everyday."

"Thank you for sharing that valuable information. Perhaps you could take over my shopping so there'd always be something handy to eat whenever you stop by. And stop giving bites to Fargo, it's bad for his teeth. And thank Janet for the scones, not me."

"Oh, testy, testy. Sorry, Fargo. Thank you, Janet. I'm glad some-one around here is aware that, unlike good wine, pastry does not improve with age."

"You're very welcome, Sonny. Enjoy. But if I were you, I would-n't get Alex started on the subject of wine."

I made a face, but actually, I loved it when she teased me. It was always mild.

"Ah, how right you are." He got up and took butter out of the fridge and smeared some on his scone. "Just thought I'd drop by with the facts, ladies, just the facts." I wished I could tell him that I could do with fewer facts and more of Janet at the moment. She had looked particularly winsome when she had kidded me about the wine. But it was not to be. Sonny was here with the facts.

"The bad news first, Alex, that sweet innocent boy you and Sergeant York managed to subdue so brutally is definitely not our murderer's accomplice, although he shows every promise of growing into one. Nasty little character. He was screaming lawsuit against you and Sergeant York for assaulting him without due cause. As opposed to assaulting him *with* due cause, I suppose. Someday if he lives long enough, he'll make an absolutely great jailhouse lawyer."

"Just what I need," I groaned. "I can see the headlines in the *Provincetown Journal* now: *Local Woman and Aging Lunatic Attack Youth In Bar.*"

"No." Sonny smiled smugly. "I counseled him wisely, and he saw the light."

"Grand. I can see more headlines: *Police Officer Accused in Cover-Up of Sister's Attack on Innocent Boy.*"

"Nothing so blatant. I just asked him if he wouldn't be mortified going into court and admitting that such a macho guy as he had been overcome by a mere female and a geriatric barfly. I also mentioned that it was sure to come out that he'd probably spent the night being naughty."

"Why does that not surprise me?"

"It developed that our pure young lad had spent yesterday evening and all night with Peter and The Wolf. He told me they had hired him to do some chores and let him spend the night on a cot in the laundry room, if you can believe that."

"Oh." Sonny and I gave each other knowing smirks. That explained a lot, including the cuff marks on the kid's wrists. But Janet again looked totally lost and we began to fill in the background for her.

"Peter Mellon and Frank Wolfman are a gay couple who run a guest house for men," I explained. "They were tagged as Peter and The Wolf by some long-forgotten wit. You'd love their house. It's a rather grand Victorian type."

"Yeah," Sonny smirked, "But it's gone a bit to seed. So have Peter and The Wolf."

I was more generous. "Well, nobody likes the thought of getting old, but it seems really to bother gay men more than most. These two came from an era when 'high camp' was the in-thing, and they never changed. They throw fancy parties, with fancy costumes and—maybe—fancy sex. But they still have a certain panache."

"They're a bit on the tatty side," Sonny concluded to Janet, "But they're not dangerous. It's just that some of their houseboys are said to do a lot more than make beds. Of course that's true of most of the B-and-Bs in town, anyway. I stopped by this morning to ask them about this new kid. The stories were much the same. The Wolf openly admitted the boy had been there, helping with some cleaning and such."

"The Wolf looks more like Ashley Wilkes on a bad day than any wolf you ever saw," I interjected.

Sonny grinned and concluded. "Wolf said they fed him and let him bunk overnight. I asked him about the restraint marks, and he suggested the kid must have gotten some caustic cleaning solution on his shirt cuffs. Nothing I can do, because the kid won't budge in his story, either. Probably afraid he'd lose his two hundred bucks."

"What will happen to him?" Janet's forehead had creased with concern.

"He did have some ID. He's one William Xavier Ambrosio from Marietta, Ohio, aged seventeen. We called his folks out there and they'll have a ticket home for him at Hyannis Airport tomorrow. We'll put him on the plane. He'll doubtless get lost somewhere or other, long before Marietta, for which the Marietta Police should send us a box of candy."

He shrugged. "William Xavier will probably have a successful career as a male prostitute until he meets someone who likes *really* rough sex. Then the River Police in New York or New Orleans or Memphis will have to deal with him. Which brings me to my second bit of news."

"That's sad," Janet said. "Even if he does think he's so tough. His family must have done something really horrible to make him run away and live like that."

Sonny sighed and grimaced. I turned my hands up in a "what can you do?" gesture. But I had dialed in on the last comment. "Second bit of news?"

"Uh huh. Guess who's in town?"

"No idea."

"The Footless Wonder. He hitched a ride."

"*What*! He hitched a *ride*? Sonny, that's not even a good joke. You mean he's *alive*?" I couldn't believe it.

"Far from it," Sonny answered. "Last night late the *Ocean Pearl* reeled in her last catch. Footless came in with it, caught in the net. Must have been one charming surprise to dump that out onto the deck after his being in the water for a good four days. Since *Ocean Pearl* was already on the way in, they didn't bother radioing the Coast Guard to come out and meet them. They just came on in to the dock early this morning and phoned us with the happy news of their unscheduled passenger."

Janet clapped a hand to her mouth and ran for the bathroom. Sonny and I looked at each other and sighed. I didn't go after her. There are times it's better to be alone.

Sonny looked thoughtful. "She really does react to anything at all about this missing foot business, doesn't she?"

"Well," I defended her. "Remember that drowned girl that floated in last year? You said half the EMTs and police force, including you, were barfing all over the beach. Maybe she saw a bad one when she was in the CG."

"Yeah. That could easily be true. You see one, you don't really feel the need to see another body that's been in the water. But I deliberately didn't get graphic." He frowned.

"Maybe she's a lady. Ladies get the vapors, asshole." I heard the toilet flush and water running into the bathroom basin. At least she was conscious! I had the fleeting and half-humorous thought that this delicate stomach of Janet's could be a real drawback in the P.I. business. Maybe she'd better stick to cooking. And I'd stick to investigating, since several people had told me my cooking was criminal.

"Quick, tell me the rest before she gets back." I spoke in a fast, low voice. "Where is he now, the morgue in Hyannis?"

"Yes. Collins Funeral Home took him down. Forensics will take a good look tomorrow," Sonny whispered back.

"Naturally, but I guess the report will be that he drowned."

"I don't think so."

"Why not? You figure he bled to death?"

"Nope." Sonny simpered and looked very knowing, and I could have slapped him when he did that.

"You want me to get on my knees and beg? Hurry up! Don't just sit there," I hissed, feeling like I was in some bad summer stock play. "How do you think he died? Or are you just being a wise-ass? After four days out there in the water what could you possibly tell?"

"We-ell-ll, you know I kinda depend on old Doc Marsten." He kept his voice low.

"Oh, God, the senile examining the decomposed for the stubborn!"

"Very literate, Alex. I'm impressed. Anyway, the Doc took a look, and guess what? Your Mr. Foot had come ashore with . . ."

Before I could make my usual disclaimer, a pale and red-eyed Janet re-entered the kitchen.

"A bullet hole in the back of his head."

# Chapter 9

As one, Sonny and I jumped to our feet, each grabbing one of Janet's arms and pushing her firmly into a nearby chair. We stood for a moment, one on either side of her, until we were reasonably sure she was not about to faint. Well, experience is a great teacher, right? And Mrs. Peres hadn't produced two dummies, had she? Sure enough, Janet turned a shade paler than she already was, and her hands were shaking, although she managed to mutter, "I'm okay, I'm okay," several times until she seemed to convince herself, if no one else. "I'm sorry to interrupt. Go ahead with your conversation, I really am all right."

"Not much more to say." Sonny shrugged and leaned back against the sink, nursing his coffee mug.

"I guess not," I agreed. "This pretty well has to be an end to it. It just about has to be some kind of drug deal gone sour. Somebody must have tried to pull a fast one around payment, or tried to sell bad stuff . . . something along those lines. No doubt the—uh, remains of the younger guy will turn up somewhere in a day or so."

"Well, apparently I'm definitely in the minority." Sonny poured himself another mug of coffee.

Between Sonny's thirst and Janet's tender tummy, I guess I could forget about *l'amour*. "Everybody shares your theory, Alex. But I still disagree. I think when forensics removes that bullet it will be a thirty-two, and it will be a perfect match with the one removed from the old man at the liquor store in Plymouth. And I think the younger guy is alive and well. I think he got safely ashore in that Zodiac and he's right here in Ptown. I know it. I feel it. I know there is something I'm still missing, but I'm that close." He held thumb and forefinger an inch apart. "Something is obvious and I just can't quite see it. But I will, believe me, I will."

Janet still looked a little green. I did not think it was time to pass the pastry around. And Sonny was definitely in one of his "stuck" modes. Somehow the day seemed headed south. "But still, Sonny, it could be drugs. Even if these two men are the ones who've been robbing stores around New England and New York, wherever . . . they could have been doing it to get money to buy drugs, couldn't they? I mean, it's no secret drugs do come in through New Bedford. Maybe they're starting up around here, too. Hell, maybe Harmon and his cronies are right. Maybe there is some 'mother ship' lurking out there."

"Well, maybe," Sonny admitted. "I know it's possible I'm completely wrong and it's just the age-old thieves-fell-out story. But as of right now, I'm still going with something much more close-up and personal. I mean, why would the two robbers need to keep robbing stores over a period of months? Once they got enough money to make an initial drug purchase, their profits from the re-sale should have been plenty to keep buying more and selling more. That's the way it works. It's just like any other product. You replenish your inventory using profits from sales."

He stretched comfortably. "Anyway, let's get off this unhappy and unproductive subject, Alex, we're ruining Janet's day. What have you two dreamed up to do on a nice, sunny morning?"

"There's a minor problem of logistics," I replied.

"Never your strong point."

"Oh, shut up. You see, both Janet and I need to go to the super-market, as you so kindly pointed out earlier. I also have to deliver Diane Miller's confidential final report and bill. Although," I added ruefully, "at this point it's about as confidential as appearing on Jerry Springer. Still, she doesn't know I goofed, and I don't want her to see someone outside her house waiting in the car, while I run in with the news that her husband has forgotten that pesky little clause about cleaving only to each other."

"Well, it might not be PC for conserving fossil fuel and working toward clean air, but why don't you just take two cars?"

"Because I don't have a car," Janet answered. Her voice was still shaky, and she still looked as if she weren't entirely with us.

Sonny looked surprised. "Oh. I just assumed you did."

"No. A friend drove me down to Provincetown last—ah, Sunday, I guess, and helped me find the little apartment. Then she drove back to Boston that night. I really haven't ever felt I needed a car in Boston. I think they are just an expensive nuisance in a big city, don't you?" She smiled at Sonny and I was relieved that she was looking less pale. Although it suited her, in some metaphysical poetic way.

"Some people feel that way," he said. "All I know is I want one when I want one. Anyway, Alex, just drop Janet at the market. Let her do the shopping while you go tell Ms. Miller that Ray has a presidential problem with his zipper." He snickered.

"Oh, Sonny, hush," I snapped. "It's bad enough I slipped the other night and told you who I was working for. Then I left the report and photos where Janet couldn't miss them. I really don't want to make it worse by laughing at them, even behind their backs. I doubt either one of them is going to find it funny. Or—or—the other person involved, either, if it ever gets that far. But your shopping idea makes sense. Is that all right with you, Janet?"

"Oh, sure, whatever is easiest," Janet answered indifferently. She was staring out the kitchen window as if she were miles away. I began to wonder if maybe someone she knew had died violently when she was a child and she might have witnessed it, or maybe she was still thinking about her dysfunctional family. Now that would depress anybody.

Sonny left shortly to do 'this and that,' he said, looking thoughtful as he gave Fargo a good-ye rumple. I made out a grocery list of essentials—dog food, beer, pastry, chips—you know, the basic food groups. Janet looked at it, shook her head in disgust, and was prompted to offer to make dinner. I leapt at the idea. Real home-cooked meals don't come my way all that often. Even when I eat at Mom's, which is fairly rare, I notice a lot of convenience and pre-cooked items that were not on our table when I was a kid. And maybe getting creative in the kitchen would make Janet forget her troubles, whatever they were.

Fargo seemed so woebegone I let him come along with us, and the three of us got into the car. As we drove across town toward the supermarket, Fargo looked mad at being relegated to the rear seat, Janet looked wan and distracted, I was less than thrilled at my impending errand. We were a sour and silent trio, and apparently not one of us felt up to any attempt to improve our mutual mood.

I dropped Janet at the market with a cryptic, "I'll pick you up in an hour." She nodded in unspoken agreement and gave a half-hearted wave. Fargo slithered into the front seat with a heavy sigh and a dirty look and I threw the car into gear with a jerk.

Diane Miller opened her door, admitting me to what was now a familiar setting. She held an armload of laundry headed to or from the washer. The little girl was cutting pages from an expensive magazine into strange shapes and snorting with pleasure as they fell to the floor. The baby was rattling his bars and shouting, "Gaaagh-ga," which seemed a logical comment on the way my day was going.

"Oh, it's you," was Diane's gracious greeting.

"Yes, indeed." I tried to smile and gave it up. "I have a report and a few photos to go over with you, Mrs. Miller. Then I think we can probably bring my activities in your behalf to a close here." God, I sounded like a barrister in a Dickens novel.

"What have you got? As if I couldn't guess. This didn't take long. I hope you've been thorough about this. Did you say you had photos?" Her eyes glinted with malice and she flashed a half smile.

"Is there somewhere we could sit down? It might be easier."

"Come this way." She dumped the laundry onto the couch, and I followed her into the kitchen, where she swept some dirty dishes into a far corner of the table and indicated a chair. I sat down, and handed her a copy of my report but gave her a brief verbal account of where I had followed Ray and whom he'd been with. I handed her the pictures in chronological order.

She flipped through them with glum disinterest until she got to the one of his kissing Marcia's hand.

"Bitch. Bastard! I'll kill him! If he wants a divorce, it's going to cost him plenty! He won't have a pair of socks left when I finish with him! And she'll be sorry. I'll name her in any divorce! And I'll sue her and get that tacky old shop and every cent she's got!" Her voice climbed to a shriek, and her daughter wandered in brandishing the scissors and looking frightened.

I gave her the sincere smile I reserve for children. "It's all right. Everything is okay," I lied in that awful oozy voice people who know nothing about kids always use when they're trying to convince them of something they, and everybody else, knows isn't true. "Mommy is just a little upset." I relieved her of the scissors none too gently and she began to wail, which upped the decimal level of her brother's cries. I was ready to admit total defeat for this day and trot to the locker room.

Diane managed a deep breath and said crisply, "Go turn on the TV for you and Kevin—I'm sorry, this is not your fault. Now you stop that yowling, this minute—would you like coffee?"

I sorted out the pronouns and said no thanks. I didn't want coffee. The way this day was going I needed a double bourbon without much ice. Dangling that thought in front of myself like a hundred-proof carrot, I began to try to wind down my connection with my client.

"Mrs. Miller, I understand your unhappiness around this situation, but that photo could merely mean that your husband paid an evening business house call to Ms. Robby. It could be that simple." I probably sounded about like I did when I was getting ready to take the scissors away from the kid.

Diane shot me a look that put a fast quietus on any further discussion along those lines. I tried a slightly different tack. "Well, even if there's a more personal relationship involved, I can't believe it's of a permanent nature. Look, how old is Ray . . . thirty-three or four?" She nodded. "Then I really can't see his leaving his wife and family to spend the rest of his life with a woman who's a good fifteen years older than he is, can you?"

Diane sniffed. "Well, maybe not. It just scares me to death. What would I do with these two kids and no father for them? And there's never enough money to go 'round if you separate! He's unhappy and always going out somewhere, even if it isn't with another woman, and I'm stuck here all the time by myself with just the kids. Sometimes I think I'll go crazy if I open one more jar of baby food. And I just about get one mess cleaned up, and one of them has made another!"

I wondered briefly if I looked like her mother, reached for a cigarette and thought I better not. I said. "Ummh," which was all it took to put the needle back on her record.

"I know things are a mess and I'm a mess and I don't blame him for not wanting to be at home, but I just can't seem to get it together anymore. You'd never believe it, but there was a time when we both were very happy with each other. We talked. We did things together. And I do still love him. I think. The bastard."

The tears rolled, and I am a sucker for tears.

"Look, Diane, this is none of my business but maybe you two should talk with a counselor. I'm sure neither of you really wants to break up a family. Maybe you could get assistance on getting somebody to help around the house or a sitter so you could both go out to dinner or away for a weekend or something. I don't think Ray really wants to leave you. If he did, he'd have picked a twenty-year-old in a tight red skirt and no bra. And I know Marcia Robby. Things may not have progressed as far as it would seem on the surface."

There. Next week I'd have new business cards printed: *Alex Peres, Private Investigator and Marriage Counselor*. Well, why *shouldn't* lesbians be marriage counselors? Priests are.

"Anyway, I think your husband is like the little boy who decided to run away from home. He just went round and round the block because he knew he wasn't supposed to cross the street."

Diane managed a smile and scooped everything back into the manila envelope. "I'll be careful what I do with this, and I'll cool down for a couple of days before I do anything. I really am not a complete imbecile, although I can't blame you for thinking that I am. Wait a sec and I'll get you a check."

She was back in a moment, and we walked together toward the door. She handed me the check. "Thanks. And I still say your prices are more immoral than the people you investigate." We grinned at each other and somehow I felt better than I had an hour ago.

In the car I looked at my watch: still a good half hour before picking up Janet. Plenty of time for that bourbon at the Rat. Fargo read my mind and laid a sorrowful head on my knee. So I speeded up and made it to Race Point in fast time and let him out. He ran at top speed along the hard-sand section of the beach, low to the ground, flat out with that beautiful power and those rippling muscles.

Watching him run was better than the bourbon would have been. While he chased imaginary prey up and down the beach, I had a cigarette. That felt good, too. Perhaps the day was salvageable after all.

I pulled up in front of the market where Janet stood waiting with a full cart of groceries and got out to help her load them in the car. Another, older, woman came through the exit at that moment. As I walked around the car both women called "Hi, Alex!" and then turned to look at each other in confusion.

I laughed. "Hello, Aunt Mae, may I introduce my friend Janet Meacham? And, Janet, meet my aunt, Mae Cartwright." The two women shook hands, and Janet looked thrilled.

"Oh, Mrs. Cartwright, I bought your two books on herbs the other day. I've skimmed through both of them, and they're just delightful. I can't wait for a rainy day to curl up and read them thoroughly."

"Well, aren't you nice!" Aunt Mae was beaming and trying to look modest at the same time and failing miserably. "Are you an herbalist?"

Janet raised a negating hand to her mouth. "Oh, goodness, no. I just love to cook with them. I know very little about them. Alex knows them much better than I do."

Aunt Mae laughed. "I find that very hard to believe."

I made a face. "Obviously, you two don't need me for a few minutes. I'll walk over and get a bottle of wine for tonight. Excuse me, ladies."

I browsed a bit and finally bought a bottle of Beaujolais. No, I didn't know what we were having for dinner, and no, I didn't care. I like red wine.

I returned just in time to hear, "Why, Janet, I would be delighted to sign the books, and yes, there is a third. It would be my pleasure to give you a copy." Apparently Janet had made a good impression.

I knew she had, when Aunt Mae continued. "Cooking with herbs is just the tip of the iceberg. For years, you know, they were our only medicines and I find that interesting—especially when one finds the same herbs used in today's commercial remedies. Of course, I don't recommend them to anyone, I'm not a doctor . . ."

Janet reached out to touch her hand. "How wise! But the history of them as medicines must be fascinating! And to realize so many of them actually worked!"

I finally cleared my throat gently.

Aunt Mae gave me one of those familial moues that meant, "Don't be so impatient." But she addressed herself sweetly to Janet. "I won't keep you girls, and I must get home. But Janet, on Monday afternoon I'm going up to Orleans to this marvelous place where they grow herbs for wholesale to retail nurseries, florists and so on."

With a broad gesture she continued. "They have thousands of plants and seedlings this time of year in their greenhouses. It's really something to see . . . and smell. I've known the owners for years—a charming couple—why don't you ride down with me and meet them? I know they'd love to show you around."

She delivered the final inducement. "You might even let me help you pick up one or two plants for a window sill. That's how I started. And food tastes so much better seasoned with herbs snipped fresh, right from the plant."

"Oh, Mrs. Cartwright, that sounds just wonderful. I've never seen anything like that greenhouse—I'm sure—it will be a real treat. Between your books and the greenhouse . . . I'm learning, I'm learning." She was ready to include me in the trip. "Alex, you're coming, of course?"

Aunt Mae laughed and answered for me. "Alexandra? All she would think to do with herbs would be sprinkle them on Fargo's food. To Alexandra the word 'cook' means some explorer who discovered Hawaii."

"I grow basil and dill every year in the back yard," I protested.

"And it took me ten years to get you to do it." Aunt Mae had settled the issue. They agreed she would pick up Janet around two on Monday at her apartment, and we parted.

Janet's mood seemed to have improved measurably. She was bubbly about meeting Aunt Mae and about the planned excursion. Fargo and I were more interested in the grocery bags with which he now happily shared the back seat. And we three arrived back at my place in considerably better humor than we had left it. We carried in the bags and Janet put aside the few items she had picked up for herself. I put away the staples. And we were all ready to begin dinner.

I soon discovered that my part in this production was apparently limited to being told to set the wine on the steps outside the back door.

I came back in and gave Janet a hug. "I'm glad to see you know that 'room temperature' for red wine doesn't mean seventy-five degrees."

"No." She shook her head. "It doesn't. The 'room temperature' that gives red wine its best taste is fifty-five degrees, which is the temperature of most old European wine cellars."

"Now where did you learn that?" I asked. "It's not common knowledge. I'm supposed to be the wine expert."

"Hah!" She began to pound the chicken breasts. "I convinced the CG to send me to cooking school. I did well and eventually became manager and head chef of the Officers' Club outside Seattle. Believe it or not, I learned it there."

"Head chef and manager! That's really something, and at your age."

"Well, I worked hard, in school and later. It wasn't exactly a Michelin five-star operation, but it wasn't at all bad. The food and presentation were considered excellent. I stayed in budget. And I got along with people. I think I would have made chief petty officer within a year."

"Did something change that?" Her eyes clouded. Anger? Hurt? I wasn't sure. "Don't get me off on that track," she said flatly. "We're planning a pleasant evening. Now let me get to work. You and Fargo—out!"

I didn't mind. I found a rerun of *The Russians Are Coming, The Russians Are Coming* on TV and settled down happily. It never failed to give me belly laughs. I've seen it so often I can quote half the dialogue. I still love it.

But simultaneously, I felt very sad for Janet. It looked as if the CG had somehow given her a raw deal, after giving her what seemed such a bright future. I wondered what on earth could have happened. Homophobia, maybe—again?

Eventually marvelous aromas began to waft in to the living room. And poor Fargo made foray after foray to the kitchen, only to be turned away each time. Finally he sat exactly one foot outside the kitchen door and alertly watched Janet's every move. If she had dropped a single bite of food, Fargo would have beaten her to it, hands down.

It was to be formal, I saw. She even set the table in my seldom-used dining area. She had taken the candelabra and tapers from the sideboard. She wiped down the good wine glasses. I said nothing, but quietly went to the bedroom and traded my sweatshirt and jeans for slacks, shirt and ascot. At last dinner was served.

She could have opened her restaurant right then and there for my money. Boneless chicken breasts on a nest of morel mushrooms and artichoke hearts with a buttery-crystallized-gingery-hint-of-thyme sauce graced my best dinner service. She had made honest-to-god homemade mashed potatoes with crumbled onion rings and a fresh fruit salad with yogurt-honey-sesame seed dressing. And we had little pieces of unsweetened cornbread with whole-kernel corn mixed in it, topped with a dollop of sweet butter.

Of course, there was also the perfect accompaniment of the Beaujolais . . . a modest little wine, yet sure-footed and aware of its own . . . well, you get the idea.

It is an old wives tale that you cannot make love on a full stomach, and like so many old wives tales, it is untrue. It *is* perhaps wise to forego dessert before making love, and we did that.

But later, around ten o'clock, we got the munchies. And damn, dessert did taste good then. Janet had had no time earlier to make anything fancy, she had said, so it was plain old vanilla ice cream with chocolate sauce served atop a slice of pound cake. Plain can be just fine, fine I say.

As we ate, Janet's thoughts returned to our conversation of earlier that day. She looked at me thoughtfully. "You have a good life, Alex."

"I've certainly had a good evening," I agreed.

"No, I'm serious. Your Aunt Mae is a pure pleasure, and you speak fondly of your mother—"

"You'll meet Mom at some point," I interjected. "She and Aunt Mae make quite the pair. They not only love each other as sisters, I think they really like each other, too. They've gotten considerably more adventurous of late. Last year they went to a dude ranch. The year before that they went to Mardi Gras. Last fall I took them to New York and they were like a couple of twenty-year-olds."

"I can believe it. Sonny's okay, too. He's not over-bearing like so many straight men. You two are fun to watch. Neither of you would ever admit it, but you really love each other deeply, you know."

"Well, I suppose perhaps we do." I licked the last of the chocolate sauce off my spoon. "Certainly we trust each other. Even when we were little kids we never ratted on each other. I know he'd be there if I hollered for help, even if he thought I was wrong. And I'd be there for him. We do best in small doses, however."

"Nothing wrong with that, it's the trust that counts, knowing he'll never let you down." It seemed to me I'd heard that phrase before. Who had it been? The parents, the CG, the lover, a friend . . . all of the above?

Janet poured us the last dollop of coffee. "And you like your job . . . actually *both* of your jobs. Your photos are wonderfully moving, even when they're humorous. They catch a spirit of animals that says you love them, love nature. Of course, you're flip about being a P.I., but I think that's because you're sensitive about it. Could I have one of your cigarettes?" I pushed the pack and lighter across the table.

"You really care about doing a good job and treating your clients properly. You sort of make fun of it to cover how hard you try. But I could see through it. You were really upset that Sonny and I knew about the Millers. I'm sorry I happened to see that stuff. I'll never say a word."

She shook out a cigarette and lit it. As she took the first drag, I reassured her.

"Of course not, I know that. And it was entirely my fault, not yours at all. The thing is—now every time you see any one of those people, you'll think of this particular time in their lives. It will change the way you look at them forever, and that's too bad. All three people in that situation were—directly or indirectly—entitled to my discretion. And I blew it. I've never done that before. I hope I don't ever do it again."

"You won't. I think you are probably the most trustworthy person I've ever met. You make me feel safe when I'm with you."

"I'm glad," I replied. "Somehow I get the idea you could use a safe harbor. Things seem to have been a little rough and stormy for you."

She smiled. "Are you offering one?"

"Could be." I took her hand. "I cannot say much for my track record. I think maybe I don't respond well to very much together-ness, although I seem to be enjoying it with you. A lot. Although, at some point, I'd still probably require considerable space, privacy. But that's not very romantic, is it? And it doesn't sound like I'm such a safe harbor, after all." I stifled a yawn.

"It's romantic enough. My track record isn't so hot either . . . as witness my recent downfall with Terry."

Terry, I thought, so you were the lover. I wonder just what happened? I re-focused on Janet's voice as she said, "I think there's only one thing that would ever make someone feel unsafe with you."

"What's that?" I sat up straight, curious.

"Your personal integrity. I have the feeling that no matter how hard it was for you—however painful—you would never let anyone infringe upon that."

I must have looked at her strangely, for she gave a little laugh and modified the statement. "I mean, what if I watered the drinks in my restaurant? Even though I'm your lover, I'll bet you would have me arrested."

"On the spot. Watering drinks is a heinous crime, punishable by immediate hanging in the public square." I considered pursuing her remark more deeply, but I was suddenly overcome by the giant yawn that had been stalking me. "My integrity forces me to tell you I'm about to fall asleep."

We both laughed. Janet carried the dishes to the kitchen while I went out on last patrol with Fargo.

And so we went happily and peacefully to bed, or at least Janet and I did. Fargo, unassuaged by his own little dish of ice cream, stirred fretfully outside the bedroom door, whuffling with disapproval. I really had to think about a bigger bed . . . maybe an added room . . . maybe two . . .

# Chapter 10

Diane Miller had had me deported to Ireland for running a TV commercial on CNN telling everyone her husband was screwing Marcia Robby in a greenhouse filled with borage. I was running lost through dark peat bogs, chased by a small child riding on a howling banshee and waving hedge clippers that glinted malevolently in the night.

Janet's sleepy voice woke me. "Alex, for God's sake see what's wrong with Fargo. He must have his tail caught." She turned over heavily, sighed and pulled the covers over her head.

Indeed he did sound *in extremis*, but I knew he really only wanted in, and consequently out. I grabbed some clothes and tip-toed for the bedroom door. As I walked across the room, the day's attire tucked under my arm, I noticed Janet's clothing, neatly folded and/or hung on a straight chair. I observed that it all looked brand new, even her bra and underpants seemed not just neat and clean but *new*.

In contrast, I looked at the two little bundles I carried. One headed for the hamper, the other clean bundle to be worn after my shower. They looked more or less alike . . . ratty. One sock had a hole in the heel and another was raveling at the top of the ribbing. A pair of underpants had a side seam opening up, and a bra was missing a hook. The outer clothing simply looked . . . worn.

It was all because I hated to shop. So when I did manage to drag myself into a store, I bought a lot all at once. Two-dozen underpants, a dozen crew socks, six bras. Maybe a half-dozen button-down oxford shirts, jeans, sweatshirts. I was well supplied for quite some time. Then one day I awoke to a choice of rags or tatters. Obviously I had reached that stage.

I showered and dressed unhappily, still thinking of my wardrobe. I let Fargo out for his morning patrol of the backyard—after many licks and wiggles of reunion following our long, sad night of separation. I put on the coffee and continued thoughts of clothing . . . this time, Janet's.

I confess I'm not always as attentive as I should be about what another woman is wearing at a given moment. This has several times caused me to be an unwilling participant in unhappy scenes, the full implicit import of which I have never truly comprehended.

But, thinking back, it seemed to me that *all* Janet's clothes I had seen in the last few days looked new. Surely, she would have brought clothes with her from Boston, wouldn't she? And nobody had all new clothes at any one time, did they? She said she was watching her money. Surely she wouldn't have replaced her entire wardrobe because of an emotional upset!

She had mentioned that she was keeping her Boston apartment for a month or so while she decided what to do with her life, but it was hard to believe she had just walked out without a change of socks. There have been occasional stretches in my life when I've wanted simply to get in the car and drive into the sunset, and once I did, but I took some clothes with me, however haphazardly selected and packed.

Maybe she and this Terry had had a fight and she'd just stormed out and then decided not to go back. Or maybe she was afraid to go back. I supposed Terry could be the violent type. At any rate, it was weird.

As I collected the morning paper and let Fargo in, I had a happier thought. Bless her heart, maybe she had bought them to impress *me*. As if she needed new clothes to do that! But it made sense in a Janet kind of way . . . new beginnings, new clothes. Well, I'd go shopping soon, too.

I poured my coffee and flipped open the paper. Israel and Palestine were again—still—talking peace and throwing bombs. The Euro was flat against the dollar, and while Brazil was looking up, Argentina was looking down. There was a possibility of a terrorist attack against overseas flights, and we were told *exactly* what counter-measures were being taken, so the terrorists were well informed of what not to do. The President assured us he had supreme confidence in an argumentative cabinet member, which was a sure sign he'd be gone by lunch. It all seemed about normal. I turned to the comics and horoscope page to provide my daily intellectual and inspirational fodder.

Leo (me) should stay in close touch with family or loved ones and not interfere in matters which did not concern them. So much for my marriage counseling plans. Aries (Fargo) should spend a pleasant day with friends and not worry about a nagging problem. It would soon be solved. Was he finally going to catch a seagull? I hoped not. "I wonder what sign Janet is?" I mused aloud.

"Scorpio," she said as she leaned over and kissed the top of my head. "And it darned well better be good."

"It says you must consider your options, stop procrastinating about important matters and put needs before pleasure. That means please pour me some coffee." I held up my mug for a refill.

"It means I have certain chores like laundry and it means I said I was coming down here to write, which I have been too busy pouring your coffee to do much of, smarty." She poured coffee for us both and sat down across from me with a smile. I could get to like this, I thought briefly. *Would* this time be different? I almost let myself believe it might.

I grinned at her. "You sound like Billie, down at the Rat, which if you're going to be a famous writer, as you are, you don't want to do much of, except for emphasis sometimes maybe. Want to go get your laundry and do it here?" I asked, thinking perhaps to prolong the unusually pleasant togetherness bit.

"Thanks but no. Mrs. Madeiros said I could use her washer and dryer. It's simpler to do it there. And I really do need some time to write, or try to write, or think about trying to write. You're not upset by that, are you?"

"Not at all. The muses must be served. Solitude is often benign. I shall simply think lovingly of you from afar. And I should be out looking for photo ops while I have time and the weather is good. It was just a thought."

Then I had a brilliant idea. I'd subtly find out if maybe she did buy the clothes to please me. After all, I'm a trained investigator. "But laundry reminds me of something else. Are you some kind of fashion model on the side or something?"

"Good God, no!" she laughed. "I feel sorry for the store that's *that* desperate! Why on earth would you think that?"

"Just idle curiosity. I happened to realize that your clothes all look new and wondered if maybe they gave them to you as part of the deal or something." Oops! I forgot that I was supposed to be curbing my curious nature.

"Oh," she looked disconcerted for a moment and then shrugged. "I picked up a few things when I first got to Provincetown . . . just to give myself a little lift, you know? I was kind of down on myself, and feeling rather bereft and worthless. And, as every woman knows, new clothes always work wonders for that. You know how that is, second only to a new haircut and massage. I have some money saved up from my Coastie days and I think sometimes it's important to sort of 'treat' yourself when you're feeling down . . .

even if you are on a budget. I think any woman is entitled just to bury the nasty old garbage that's been making her sad and turn into a brand new woman, wardrobe and all. Do you agree?"

"Oh, yes, indeed. I just wondered. And I think you could be a model, anyway." So much for the clothes. But at least it settled the question I'd been harboring about how she was going to get along financially. I felt a little foolish even bringing it all up and changed the subject awkwardly. "Several days ago I promised my mom I'd come for dinner tonight. If you'd like to come along with me . . ." Oh, God, what am I saying? I've known her four days—I don't think I've even mentioned her name to Mom. Oh, God.

"Aren't you sweet. Thank you, but I really just do need to be quiet tonight. I feel like so much good and bad has been happening to me lately." She paused for a sip of coffee. "Completely rearranging my life, moving down here, trying to find out if I'm a writer. And meeting you—that's the good part, of course. But it's all been unbelievably stressful for me. I need a little downtime to absorb it all, even the lovely part. Can you promise me a raincheck with your mom? I really do look forward to meeting her."

"Sure. I just wanted you to know you'd be welcome." Truth to tell, I was more than a little relieved. An incidental meeting with Aunt Mae was one thing. Taking Janet home to 'meet mother' was something I wasn't quite ready for, although I couldn't really think of a reason why. Janet was presentable, polite, well mannered, intelligent. And she was certainly looming ever larger in my life. Maybe that was the problem. I tended to get nervous when people loomed. Well, I didn't have to deal with that right now. We lingered over coffee, agreed that Janet would call me tomorrow and we would decide then what we wanted to do for the day. With all my talk of not wanting to be in anyone else's pocket, I noticed I hadn't suggested that we spend the day apart.

The phone rang, and as I picked it up, Janet left the kitchen to get dressed. It was Sgt. Peres, of Provincetown's finest. We chatted for a few moments about Mom's upcoming birthday and what we might combine to get her. I told him I'd be at Mom's tonight. He said he'd try to be there, too. Then he got to the real reason for his call.

"The footless wonder finally has a name. At the morgue yesterday they found a wallet zipped inside a pocket of his jacket, and in the wallet was a driver's license still dry enough to decipher, even after all its time in the water. Footless, we now pretty safely assume, is one Mr. Maynard Terrence O'Malley, hailing from scenic Stonington, Connecticut."

"From Connecticut?" I was surprised. "I thought the plates on the car were from New Jersey."

"They were stolen, remember?"

"Oh, yeah, I forgot about that. Have the Stonington Police been able to track O'Malley down? Did they come up with anything about his background or a mysterious dark-skinned buddy?"

"Nothing came up yet about the second man. But they did locate O'Malley's mother, living at the address in his wallet. They say she's pretty much the ditsy type, along with being very upset about his death, of course. She says he really didn't live there with her for several years, just used the address because he sort of moved around a lot."

"I'll bet he just did, with his career in robbery and other lovely hobbies."

"Yes. She told Stonington he spent most of his time in Bridgeport, or was it Norwalk? No, maybe it was Stamford."

"If it wasn't Hartford or New Haven," I completed.

"You got it. I don't think anybody's going to get much help from her, poor thing. She also informed them that your Maynard . . ."

"He is not my Maynard, or my anything else, dammit!"

"Oh, I keep forgetting. I thought it was finders' keepers. Anyway, she advised Stonington that he stayed in *whatever* city with his girl-friend, who may possibly be named—get this one—Jane Peaches!"

"Or Suzy Strawberry," I added.

"Or Eloise Eggplant."

107

"Or Calliope Cantaloupe."

Sonny giggled and then deepened his voice. Someone must have come into his office. He cleared his throat. "So-oo-o, things are beginning to move a little. We hope to have somebody up in Hyannis Monday to make a positive ID."

"Won't fingerprints do it?" Then I realized maybe he was one of the many who'd never had reason to be fingerprinted.

"Can't get any, the flesh is too decomposed and too nibbled by the itty bitty fishies in the gweat big pond."

"Aaargh. But surely they're not going to bring that poor nutty mother up here to ID him after he spent four days in that pond!"

"No way. Anyhow, he's unrecognizable, even to a mother. They're trying to see if he's got a dentist down there, and they'll bring him up. Be a shame to pull the poor bastard away from an eight-hundred dollar root canal, wouldn't it? Well, just thought I'd update you. Hug Fargo. I gotta go, I've got another call." He rang off.

Janet had come back into the kitchen about halfway through the conversation and started straightening things up. "More news?" she asked. Once again she seemed a bit pale to me, but I put it down to lack of makeup. Makeup or no makeup, she was lovely to look at.

"Yeah. They think our footless man is now identified as one Maynard Terrence O'Malley from Connecticut."

"Well, faith and begorrah! What a good Irish name! They just do keep cropping up in this little mystery."

"Don't they! The more I think about it, the more sense it makes. McKinney or someone hires O'Malley and his buddy to 'steal' his boat and deliver the arms to a ship. While they're killing time around Plymouth, waiting for the storm to blow out, they pick up a little extra cash from the robberies. Then they head to sea and, as the tabloids will say, to their fatal rendezvous."

I had a delicious thought. "Do you realize we may just have solved a mystery that about five law enforcement groups are running in circles trying to get a handle on?" I exclaimed.

"Wouldn't that be perfect! The women do it again! And amateurs, at that! Oh, I do hope you're right," I raised my coffee cup in a toast.

We both laughed and parted affectionately, and I was torn between feeling a little bereft and a little liberated. I wasn't particularly happy with either feeling, so I collected camera and gear plus dog and headed for the piney woods.

I parked by the side of the road. Fargo and I walked in along one of the bike paths, our footfalls silent on the cushion of fallen needles, looking for scenes or natural vignettes that I could turn into pictures. I got a great one of Fargo, standing on his hind legs with front paws leaning against a tree trunk, stretched to his full sleek, muscular height. Above him, head-down on the tree was a squirrel, nose not two inches above Fargo's. I swear they were both laughing. I may blow that one up and give it to Sonny for his birthday. Or I may sell it. More likely both.

We strolled on and I made another shot or two. A bunch of grackles gathered ominously on the limbs of a dead tree like the crows on the Capitoline steps, a pair of late-staying rosy grosbeaks scratching for food by an ilax bush, their pompous round breasts and short busy beaks reminding me of two matrons gossiping over tea. I was quite pleased, but you can never really be sure until they're developed.

We circled back to the road and Harmon careened by in his old rattletrap truck, waving furiously. I waved back and was immediately thirsty. We drove back into town and parked on Commercial Street. You can do that easily this time of year and I relish it while I can. I gave Fargo his drink in the car and he allowed me to go in and get mine.

I picked up a beer at the bar and walked over to the table that was my 'other office.' It was fun to eavesdrop on the other drinkers, as usual. Today, of course, the conversation was all about the body brought in by the *Ocean Pearl*. According to the local pundits, a full-scale drug war was breaking out. It would not be safe for boats to leave the docks. It would not even be safe for people to walk the streets. The FBI was coming *en masse* to protect civilians.

Just to add a little fuel to their fire, I solemnly recounted Janet's recent IRA gun-running theory. It was kerosene on a smoldering ember. Some of them went running full tilt after this new, intriguing flame, while others vigorously defended the ever-popular traditional drug theory. It should keep them going happily, long into the night.

In a few minutes Joe brought me another beer. As he plunked it before me he shook his finger in a pretend-warning. "Now, lissen here, Alex, you got to stop beating up on my male customers. Looks bad—a woman whomping on a man."

"Better than the other way round, Joe. Anyway, that was no man, that was just a brat. Brats are open season."

He tucked his bar cloth in his belt. "Well, I'll let it go just this once, if you promise to lay off that Women's Lib with Billie. She's hard enough to live with as it is."

"Billie is a jewel beyond value, Joe. You should treasure her with every breath. Anyhow, she makes the best crab cakes in Massachusetts."

"Now you finally got it right." He patted me on the shoulder and walked away.

Real good ol' Amurrcan bar humor. I was relaxed and happy, without a caveat anywhere in my mind, which I find is often a mistake.

I figured two beers had better be it, since I was shortly going to my mother's. So I downed the last of it and settled up. As I went up the alley toward the street an apparition of arms and fists and elbows leaped out at me from behind Jacobs' Gift Shoppe. Instinctively I jumped back and therefore avoided the first clumsy onslaught of Ray Miller and was well prepared for the second.

"I'll fix you for fucking up my life!" he screamed, aiming a wobbly punch at my chin. Ray was not a pugilist.

I simply grabbed his arm and swung, using his own momentum to spin him around and into the wall of the Jacobs' store. His back hit it with a resounding thud, and I hoped they had left no glassware on the shelves when they closed for the winter. He slid slowly down to a sitting position and stared fixedly at his left shoe. I stood over him till he tried to get up, at which point I kicked his feet out from under him, just to get his attention.

"Stay down, Ray, or we'll have to do this again and the second time it might hurt. Are you hearing me?" He gave a small nod and I continued. "First of all, I didn't fuck up your life, you did. Secondly, just answer me one question. Do you want a divorce?" He stared up at me with his mouth open and eyes wide with amazement. "Not from me, you idiot, from Diane!"

"Yes. No. I don't guess so. I don't know."

"Typical of incisive male thinking when it comes to anything involving the emotions, Ray!" I found that I was getting angry, not so much at his trying to hit me, but for his treatment of Diane that had resulted in his attack on me. "Uncross your eyes and listen to me, Romeo."

He made a face and lifted his hands palm-up in surrender.

"Ray, do you know that Diane spends all day everyday with one kid who wets his pants and another who thinks she's Salvador Dali? These are her *only* companions! Her *only* intellectual stimulation. You, on the other hand, put on a nice suit every morning and toddle off to solve the world's financial problems, go to lunch with a client or friends, kid around with two secretaries or assistants or whatever they are and then finally wander home, where your shirts are clean and ironed and another suit is pressed for tomorrow. The house is a mess, Diane is a mess, the kids are clean enough but edgy and whiny. But your fucking shirts are ironed and your fucking dinner is on the table so you can eat and go out drinking with your buddies or go drool all over Marcia and tell her how misunderstood you are."

I was obviously getting madder by the minute, and Ray was looking up at me with some alarm. "Ah, Alex, I didn't mean to cause so much . . . you know I would never hurt Diane . . ."

"The hell you wouldn't! Shut up and listen to me, you miserable slimy slug. You've got a good business. It certainly supports your nights out with the boys and your expensive little gifts to Marcia."

111

That was a shot in the dark, but his face told me I hit the mark. "So you just take some of that money and hire Diane a part-time sitter or housekeeper so she can get out of that house and have her hair done or have lunch and shop or something. And then you get *another* sitter and take her out to dinner or away for a weekend. And pay some attention to your kids. For all I know, they might even be cute if the whole household wasn't too depressed and angry to notice they're alive!"

I leaned over and tapped his chest with my forefinger. "*Do it*, Ray, or so help me, I'll fake a photo that looks like you sneaking out of Peter and The Wolf's at five a.m., and I'll nail it to every phone pole in town!" With that cheery thought I left him. He'd gone back to staring at his shoe.

I got to the car to find that Fargo had slept through the entire scene, which made me wonder what he might do if Ray came by to burn the house down at midnight. But I was too pleased with myself to dwell on it. I had struck a mighty blow in the cause of woman-hood. And maybe I'd get those business cards reprinted after all. Huzzah!

I went home and showered and dressed to go to Mom's, but realized I was a little early. So I said the hell with it and had another beer and thought about how clever I was while I watched Tiger Woods start to blow another tournament away.

Then Fargo and I began our walk over to my mother's house. He was pleased, either at the walk or because he knew where he was going. He knew he'd be coddled and cuddled and fed to the gills. Well, I thought, we were both following our horoscopes for the day. He'd been with his squirrel-friend earlier and didn't seem to have a care in the world now that he had me to himself. Uh-oh, was *that* his nagging problem? Well, it was solved for tonight, anyway. And I'd been with Janet earlier and would be with Mom, and there you were. Whoever said horoscopes were garbage?

Horoscopes. Zodiacs. What was it with the damn Zodiacs? What was wrong with them? Then my dream came back to me, as clear as the instant replay in a televised football game. Yes! Janet had said it in my dream. "I should know what a Zodiac is. I was an admiral in the Coast Guard." Of course! It was the night I had met Janet and Sonny had come into the Rat to tell me they had found the Bertram cruiser, but the Zodiac that should have been in tow was missing. Janet had seemed not to know what a Zodiac was—the boat Zodiac, that is. In fact she had made some silly reference to a horoscope at the time.

My walk slowed almost to a halt as I thought. God, the Coast Guard used Zodiacs all the time, probably had dozens—maybe hundreds—of the damn things. As an ex-Coast Guardsman, how could she not know what they were? Well, now slow down, Alex. At that time, she had just heard about a murder and a messy death, had just come to from a faint in a strange place, surrounded by people she had never even seen before, one of them a cop in full regalia. Doubtless she was confused, embarrassed, maybe even a little frightened. She just got it garbled up at the moment. She probably just said it to have something to say.

I was sure that was it. Coincidence was all. But I didn't think Maynard Terrence O'Malley's name was a coincidence. Now that had possibilities! I wondered if Sonny had learned anything during the day. I hoped he'd be home for dinner so I could hear the latest.

Fargo pulled on the leash and I speeded up. Both of us were hungry, as we approached the house. Like most Ptown houses and yards, Mom's was neat and well kept. The straight-up two-story house was a New England style in pale yellow with maroon shutters. The front yard was tiny, with just enough room for some flowers in season and enclosed by a picket fence and gate—painted white, of course.

Like most people I ignored the front door and went up the driveway, past the small side yard with its shade tree and picnic table and benches, and into the larger backyard. I opened the backdoor to my mother's house and called, "Hi, Mom, I'm here!" as I had done so often all my life. Wherever I lived, I knew this house would always, on the bottom line, be home.

113

I caught the marvelous aroma of sausage and kale soup and fresh-baked homemade rolls. I love my mother, of course, but somehow my feelings seem even more affectionate at times like this. I gave her a kiss. She was edging toward sixty. Her once-auburn hair now had enough white in it to appear ash-blonde. But her figure was still good. She had on jeans and a man-tailored lavender shirt with the sleeves rolled up. She seemed younger than her years. And a splash of flour on one cheek simply gave her a rakish look.

"There's my big baby boy!" she crooned to Fargo. "Is he a hungry fellow? Well, he shall have his own special bowl of soup."

"How about me?" I asked.

"Oh, you, you'll eat anything." She smiled and patted my arm with a trace less enthusiasm than she had patted Fargo. I tried not to be jealous.

"I'm an adult, I can take this," I pouted.

"Now, darling, don't be silly. You can have your special bowl of soup, too. Are you hungry? It's all ready. And I made an apple pie."

Already I felt better. "Should we wait for Sonny? Is he coming home? He said he'd try to make it." I hadn't seen his car in the driveway.

Mom glanced out the kitchen window. "He's pulling in right this minute."

He walked into the kitchen shedding his jacket and tie and draping them over a chair. Mom gave me a roll-eyed look and handed them back to him. Sighing, he put the tie in the jacket pocket and hung the jacket in the hall closet. Then he opened us both a beer and we sat at the kitchen table as we had on so many evenings of our childhood—minus the beer, of course—facing each other across the waxed white oak table while Mom busied herself at the stove.

Dining rooms were for birthdays and holidays and company. We sipped our beers in silence for a few minutes, while I gave him time to start to relax.

Then I said, "Hey, Sonny, Janet came up with an intriguing point regarding Mr. Footless, a.k.a. Mr. Maynard Terrence O'Malley, good Irishman that he is . . . was. There are getting to be several

Irish involved here. It seems really possible to me that McKinney made his boat available in some way to the two thugs. Either O'Malley and friend got into a fight before they ever got to the ship, or maybe somebody on the ship didn't want to pay them or maybe O'Malley doubled the price at the last minute. Perhaps even the FBI was on board the ship and now everything is a big cover-up. It makes sense, you know." I stopped, out of breath.

Sonny leaned back in his chair as Mom served the yummy-smelling soup. He swallowed a spoonful and winced at the heat and took a gulp of beer. "It's a thought. Usually, though, the IRA does-n't do or even talk much in America about guns. It's pretty much only the political wing of the IRA over here, and they like to come across as gentle, peace-loving fellas who just raise a little money to help the orphans and widows left by the mean, cruel Brits. Of course they take the money they collect in America and buy the guns from Syria or Libya, but we aren't supposed to know about that."

"They never ship guns from here?" I couldn't believe it.

"Well, hardly ever," he grinned.

"And now you are the master of the queen's nav-vee," Mom interposed. "Eat your soup before it's cold."

"Aye, aye, ma'am. Actually, Alex, we should know more very shortly. Chief Wood said he'd stop by about now on his way home from the station.

"I think Janet and I were quite clever to think of it. Don't you?"

"Yeah. Clever, indeed. I wasn't thinking along those lines at all. Mom, was that apple pie I smelled when I came in?"

One thing you could say about Detective Sergeant Peres, his priorities were always in order. At that moment a car door slammed, followed by Chief Wood's solid tread across the back porch.

"Come on in, Carl," my mother called.

"Jeanne, you get prettier every time I see you!" He gave her a peck on the cheek.

"Liar. How's Martha?"

"She's fine. So are the kids. Eileen's expecting her first. Carl, Jr. graduates the Academy this June if God is very good." My mother laughed. "Don't laugh, Jeanne, last year he had the dubious distinction of being eighty-two in a class of eighty-seven."

Sonny stood and the two men shook hands. "Don't worry, Carl, until he's eighty-seven in a class of eighty-two. Then you got a problem."

Mother offered coffee and a slice of pie and was accepted all around.

"Well, Carl," Sonny said between bites, "If you have any news, don't be bashful. Alex is positive we've stumbled onto some big-time arms deal here. Have we?"

Chief Wood gave me a wink. "Well, I suppose we might have. There were five ships in this general area at about the right time that night. One was a little coaster headed from Bridgeport to Portsmouth, so I crossed her off. One was a big Exxon supertanker. I didn't think she or her captain fit the bill for a side business of running arms. Neither did a Moore-Mack container ship. That left a small tanker out of Venezuela, headed for Scotland and a Swedish freighter headed home to Malmo."

"Those two sound interesting," I put in.

"Yes," Wood nodded. "Actually either of them could plan to secretly put into a small Irish harbor en route to their published destination or have a meeting set up near the coast of Ireland to off-load easily enough. They're not on the kind of schedule and set course the big tanker or container ship would be. The Venezuelan tanker especially interests me. If she met the Bertram the night of the storm, she could have dumped some oil when the Bertram was alongside, which would have smoothed out that sea for her."

He wiped his mouth almost delicately. "That sea bothers me. Transferring cargo from the Bertram to any other vessel would have been a real bitch—excuse me, Jeanne—in that weather. A twenty-eight-footer would have been bouncing like a ping-pong ball. If they had any sense they wouldn't have tried."

"Would it have even been possible?" Sonny asked.

Wood nodded. "Marginally. It would, however, explain what happened to the Bertram later. She could have taken a sideswipe from the larger ship and opened a seam the two men were unaware of. It eventually got too big for the bilge pumps to handle and she began sinking. I think the bigger guy maybe fell overboard trying to get the Zodiac started, and the little guy fell in trying to help him. Or maybe the little guy got away in the Zodiac after all, but I've got a feeling about that." The Chief looked smug.

"You look like you know something." I smiled at him.

"I don't know. But I think if anyone even tried to transship any goods that night, it must have been terribly important to them. I don't believe the Bertram would have even left harbor in that weather to deliver a couple of dozen rifles and some ammo. I think they had one, maybe two, handheld anti-tank or surface-to-air rocket launchers and ten, maybe twelve missiles for them. Wherever they picked them up, disassembled they would have fit in the back of the Acura. They would have been manageable for two men to carry and they would have fit right into the cockpit of the Bertram. And they'd be worth a *helluva* lot to somebody."

The Chief leaned forward earnestly. "They would also be a matter of great secrecy. I think whoever was behind this, told the captain of the larger ship to make sure the Bertram took some damage. I wouldn't be surprised to learn—although we'll never find her—that her bilge pumps were sabotaged. And I'd be willing to bet that Zodiac gas tank was dry from the get-go. I do not believe the two men were meant to return alive. I think they were both to disappear at sea."

After a long silence, Sonny asked quietly. "What do you think we should do?"

The Chief took the last bite of his pie and carefully folded his napkin. "Well, outside of their robbery activities, which are not a federal problem, we don't have the slightest proof of anything. I checked. The two ships are not on the Coast Guard or FBI watch-list, although a ship owned by the same company as the tanker did get involved with some Chinese illegal immigrants down in Baja."

"Oh, yes," I inserted brightly. "Sonny fears that sort of crime wave might happen right here in Provincetown."

Sonny gave me a murderous glare. Chief Wood gave Sonny an amazed look and continued. "I think for now let's leave it between us and not involve anyone officially, especially the Frozen Brains, Inc. I have a good friend in Customs. I'll ask him to ask some of his friends across the Pond to give these two ships a close look when they dock, maybe think up some reason for a board-and-search before they dock. Customs people and coastal patrols all over are pretty good at finding things or traces of things, especially when they know what to be alert for. I'll let you know."

He looked at his watch and stood. "Jeanne, that pie was pure ambrosia. Just please don't tell Martha I had it before my dinner."

He patted me on the arm, and I said, "Give my best to Mrs. Wood and all the little splinters."

The Chief, Mom and I all roared. Then Chief Wood chuckled, "I had forgotten all about that."

Sonny looked bewildered and I explained. "When I was about six, two friends and I heard that phrase on TV or somewhere and thought it terribly funny. We called the Chief's wife on several occasions, and when she would answer the phone, we would say, 'Hello, Mrs. Wood. How are you and all the little splinters?' Then we would collapse, howling with our cleverness."

I looked at Mom. "Of course, we were caught. We were grounded, and our allowances were docked so we could buy Mrs. Wood a bouquet at the supermarket. We had to walk all the way out to their house to deliver the flowers and our apologies. She accepted both and then, angel that she is, took us all to Dairy Queen before she drove us home."

"Very nice of her," Sonny agreed. "And she hasn't changed a bit over the years. Neither, I might add, have you, Alex."

Following that note of brotherly love, Sonny announced. "If you'll excuse me, I have to go look over some notes. I'm in court tomorrow morning on a hit-run case." He gave a surprisingly grace-ful Elizabethan courtier's bow and made his exit.

Chief Wood kissed Mom lightly, gave me a two-finger salute and left, grinning.

I turned to Mom. "Here, let me give you a hand clearing up. Then I better mosey along, too."

But she sat down at Sonny's place, propped her elbows on the table, laced her fingers and gave me an impish grin.

"Not so fast, young lady. Now just who is Janet?"

I folded back into my chair, laughing helplessly. She was my Mom. I told her.

# Chapter 11

Some facts in life are incontrovertible. All baby animals are adorable, even the ugly ones—maybe especially the ugly ones. The person sitting behind you in the theatre will be a compulsive talker. The person standing ahead of you in any line will encounter a problem. The person sitting beside you in the plane will have a heavy cold. Big snowflakes falling in a still night are magic. A goodly portion of Sunday belongs to the *New York Times*.

There are several reasons that make it worthwhile paying an outrageous price for the pleasure of lugging home a four-pound newspaper. It's not simply the news coverage. It's the Arts & Leisure section. It's the Book Review and the Travel section, which never fails to amaze me with all the places I do not care to visit. And, there's my personal favorite—the Magazine section.

I usually enjoy at least one of the main articles, and the fashion and home decorating pages are always good for a deep chortle of disbelief. Behind them comes Food. Usually a terribly artistic photo, which of course I find of interest, and three or four remarkable recipes. The only recipe I ever tried—scallop cakes—fell apart. Still, I love to read it. It's probably the only place in the world where you read things like, "Separate one dozen eggs and whisk the yolks lightly by hand." And recipes call for things like lemon curd and marmite, things I wouldn't know where to find, nor recognize if located.

The penultimate pleasures of the Magazine Section are the upscale real estate ads for properties around the globe, most with intriguing blurry little photos. Every week I reward myself by 'buying' the property of my choice. Last week I skipped quickly over a '$5.1 mil' penthouse overlooking Central Park and went for a '$3.8 mil' 50-acre farm outside Charlottesville, with horse barn, tennis court, guest cottage, small lake and 12-room colonial brick house. I don't play tennis—but, hell, I could always plant geraniums. This week I feel European. We'll see.

And, finally, on the next-to-last page, the *piece de resistance*! The Crossword Puzzle. A guaranteed hour and a half of the witty, the obscure, the obvious, the frustrating, tormenting, challenging, sweat-provoking, humiliating—pure delight.

With all those treats in mind, I saddled up Fargo and we set off for the only store in town that sells both the *Times* and homemade pastry. Fortunately, it was not terribly far away. The *Times* really could get heavy. We were early, but still encountered a few other people on the way.

One older woman gave us a fearful glance and stepped into the street to avoid passing within reach of Fargo. A balding man approached, head down, threw us a furtive look and crossed the street, glancing back and muttering. I wondered what his problem was. Fargo grumbled in his throat and I tightened his lead, which just made him all the grumpier. Obviously he didn't like the man's looks either. A good-looking young man smiled at us and said, "Hello there, sweet thing." I assumed he meant the dog but smiled back and said good morning anyway.

At the store I picked up the paper, a French cruller and an almond croissant to die for and a rawhide for Himself. I nodded to a real estate agent who should probably be in jail for gross misrepresentation and said "Hi" to a young woman who worked in the bank, whose name, I remembered belatedly, was Florence.

The social hour completed, Fargo and I walked home via the bayside beach. The fog was still heavy, but the sun was trying and in an hour or so would succeed. For now the air was dank and chill and hushed. Even the water was barely moving, just giving the occasional, almost silent nudge to remind the shore it was still there. We were joined for a few minutes by the frenetic little dachshund, whose name I had learned was Toby. We were both rather relieved when he turned his short bantam legs for home, his fat little bottom bouncing saucily across the sand.

Arriving home slightly damp and hungry, we settled in. I shared my pastry. Fargo made no offer to share his rawhide. I was deep into the puzzle when Sonny called.

"Sorry to bother you early, But Bob Reynolds just called me from Plymouth. Much as I hate to admit it, this Irish thing gets curiouser and curiouser."

"What happened?"

"Well, Bob checked around the area. Neither of the McKinneys hangs out at the Irish pubs, or belongs to any Irish clubs—I'm sure they are above all that. But just on a hunch, Bob talked to a couple of travel agents and with one he struck oil. About five years ago the McKinneys both went on a tour of Wales and King Arthur country, whatever that may be. About halfway through, they left the tour and took a ferry from Wales to Ireland. It's about a six-hour sail, which is one hell of a long ride, but of course ferries are pretty anonymous in case you should be looking for that. Or maybe there's just a limit to the charms of Wales, who knows."

He sneezed. "I hope I'm not getting something. Anyway, three years later Mrs. McKinney joined a tour to London without her husband. Something called Dinner and Drama, where you go to a different restaurant and see a different play or opera every night. No wonder McKinney stayed home. Well, after three nights, Mrs. McK. pulled out and flew to Dublin. The travel agent remembers both incidents because she was also the tour guide."

I took the last crumb of cruller. "Mrs. McKinney must have told the tour guide some reason for leaving."

"All the guide remembered was it was something about family. And here's a note that makes it even more interesting. Since the ferry and the plane trip were within the British Isles, it's considered domestic travel, like going from Massachusetts to New Hampshire. It does not show on your passport, so theoretically nobody knows you went there if you come back and leave the country from a regular international airport like Heathrow. Intriguing, what?"

'Sonny, do you think you should go to the FBI with this?

"I'm not sure. We have a day or so before those ships dock, although an offshore rendezvous could happen anytime, I guess. I'm going down to Connecticut in a little while to talk to O'Malley's mother. I can't believe she's as nutty as they say. If I get zilch, I guess we call the Fibbies. I can't make up my mind. This feels like a Jack Higgins novel to me. Anyway, I'll be in touch."

I looked at my watch and was surprised at how early it still was. It occurred to me that a certain straightening of the house was probably in order, since Janet would almost certainly be coming over at some point. It also occurred to me I had been doing a helluva lot of straightening and cleaning and changing of linens of late. Not that Janet wasn't worth it. Of course she was, but it might be nice to go to her place once in a while. I'd have to work on that. However, I did the housework, minimally, and told myself I didn't mind. The hell I didn't. The place did look better and smelled fresher and I did prefer it that way. I just didn't like the process of making it that way.

A beer was definitely in order, but in view of the early hour I sat down at the kitchen table to another coffee and one of the allowed cigarettes (I was still under five for the day, so buzz off). I checked my watch again and had an absolutely brilliant idea. According to the early morning weather forecast, today would become unseasonably warm ahead of a cold front due to move through the area tonight. Sunny and unseasonably warm—sounded like perfect picnic weather to me!

Janet was supposed to call me around eleven. God, I wished she'd get her phone in. The lack of it was becoming a real nuisance. She was going to get one ordered for her apartment this week, she said. I hoped there'd be no delay in installing it. Anyway, with luck I could have everything put together for the picnic and be at her apartment well before eleven. The fact that a picnic on the beach would not involve ruining the recent and unaccustomed neatness of my own house had absolutely nothing to do with it. Absolutely nothing. Sometimes my subtle cleverness amazed even me! I headed for the shower and fresh clothes, hopefully without holes.

I dragged out the cooler and put in a six pack of Bud plus two bottles of claret—an unassuming, sound little wine with overtones of a thoroughbred . . . well, no time for that. I put the cooler in the car, along with an old beach blanket. I called the Lazy Dog Cafe and asked them to put up an order of their fresh, lush lobster salad and macaroni salad (which is actually al dente, rather than the consistency of oatmeal, as you find in most restaurants), four of their little cucumber and water cress sandwiches on dark, dark pumpernickel bread and four giant date and walnut cookies. Then I put cooler, blanket, Fargo's water, a thermos of coffee, Fargo and me into the car and raced for the A&P.

There I pushed the cart swiftly up and down, purchasing a bag of ice, a chunk of Brie, crackers and six big, gorgeous peaches imported from Israel that were so expensive I didn't even worry about it. I even picked up a bunch of early daffodils to make Janet smile on this early spring day. On to The Lazy Dog Restaurant, where my order awaited me, and finally to Janet's place went Chef Peres and her trusty helper Le Fargo.

Janet saw me pull into the driveway and came out to meet me. I handed her the flowers, which indeed made her smile and touch my cheek lightly, and explained my genius idea for a picnic.

124

She was delighted until she looked into the cooler. "My God, Alex, are we going somewhere to stay for a week? If we have to carry that cooler more than six feet we'll both have permanent back damage. Let's see if we can't lighten it a little."

She rummaged through all my goodies and made a little pile of what she thought we could spare. "Four beers and one bottle of wine should be plenty unless we plan to get plastered. And we can save the peaches and Brie and crackers to have later this evening, can't we? Okay, that should help at least a little."

We carried the overage into the apartment and I put the beers and cheese in the fridge and the wine on the counter. I stepped into the central room and looked around. The apartment had been formed by the simple expedient of putting up a wall to block off the other half of the garage. There was the minute kitchen, a door leading no doubt to an equally-sized bathroom and what looked like a sizeable closet. That was it.

The furnishings were typical of inexpensive rentals all over town: a studio couch, easy chair, coffee table, a minuscule old *escritoire* with a wobbly little chair, a table in front of the big window with three straight chairs. But the covers on the furniture were crisp and clean, the walls newly painted. Aside from a really ghastly sailing ship struggling on an angry, lurid sea, it was a pleasant place.

At Janet's hands the flowers had gone quickly into a tall glass and onto the low table. The peaches then appeared on the window table in a large bowl. She put her fists on her hips and looked around. "That's better. At least there's something a little individual in here now. Before, it looked more impersonal than military quarters."

"Didn't you have your own quarters in the CG?" I asked. I was still curious about what happened during her stint with them.

"Oh, sure, after I got a few stripes. But it was still government-issue furniture, light beige walls . . . you know. I didn't have many things of my own, so it was a bit bare."

"But you were content enough?" I pursued.

"Oh, yeah. I guess so. Hush about the CG, Alex. We're going on a picnic!" She grabbed my hand and we ran down the driveway. We were on our way.

As we drove up Route 6 to Truro, I told Janet of Chief Wood's visit and the possibilities it opened up, particularly when combined with the information from Sonny's call this morning. She seemed quite excited by the news. She was glad the police weren't sitting on their collective duffs. She was pleased Chief Wood had been helpful, hoped his contacts with Customs agents would be the same. She was speaking fast, and her eyes seem so bright as to be almost feverish. I hoped she and Sonny were not coming down with something. I'd be almost sure to follow, after all.

We turned off the main road toward the lighthouse and ocean, angling left of the lighthouse and down a road that dead-ended at a fairly high bluff with steps leading down to the beach. Janet took the blanket, I picked up the thermos and we both grabbed a handle of the cooler. It was still heavy, but we managed the steps and staggered a few hundred feet around a curve in the beach to a small inlet. We immediately collapsed onto the blanket and opened two of the beers.

It was a perfect day with startlingly warm sun and almost no wind. The ocean sparkled with telegraphic dots of sunshine on the few whitecaps way off shore. Just enough surf kah-wooshed at our feet to let us know the Atlantic really was still an ocean. Not surprisingly, our mood turned amorous and we began to make love.

I think it's always exciting to make love in a strange place—I mean someplace other than your own bed. And today my excitement was augmented by that little *frisson* of concern that at any moment a hiker could appear around the bend or a boat come sailing into the cove. The feeling of the moment obviously affected Janet, too. She gave of herself avidly, with almost aggressive responses and was eagerly demanding in her turn. Finally we crossed a finish line that left us both panting and exhausted. We lay on the blanket, barely touching, and the mild breeze felt welcome on my overheated body.

Minutes later she propped up on her elbow and her fingers gently stroked my neck and shoulders. I closed my eyes in pure sensuous enjoyment of the moment. "I love you, Alex."

I opened my eyes, the moment altered. I knew what I was supposed to reply, but my tongue felt like a wooden ruler. I did manage to reply, "I love you, too, Janet." I only hoped the words didn't sound as strained coming out as they felt! What the hell was wrong with me? I did love her. At least I thought I did. What was there not to love? All of a sudden, I had that feeling again. Wrong. Here I was, cagey as usual of anything that smacked of commitment. But, try as I might, I couldn't turn off the little tinkling alarm bells. The breeze felt chill now and I felt restless, edgy.

Ah, the hell with it. I wasn't going to let my problems around intimacy ruin our day—perhaps our future!

I took her hand and kissed it softly, letting my gaze caress her body. "Much as I'm enjoying this particular view, it's a little early in the season for going starkers, isn't it? We should probably get some clothes on before we get chilled and catch a cold."

She laughed and shook her head. "Alex, Alex, you old fashioned goose. You don't catch cold from being chilly."

"I know that. Intellectually, I know for a fact that a cold is a virus, spread by droplet infection. Emotionally, I tell you my grandmother was right all along. Catch a chill, catch a cold. Anyway, I'm starved. Let's eat."

We got dressed. I stayed barefoot for the first time that year. Janet put on her sneakers, explaining that if she stayed barefoot she would assuredly find the one sharp shell on the beach and cut her foot.

"Like I unerringly step on the one icy spot on the sidewalk," I smiled.

"It's good to know you're not perfect."

"I'm workin' on it."

We ate like trenchermen, hardly speaking, making little groans of pleasure at the big bites of succulent seafood and crisp sandwiches, taking unaesthetic gulps of wine to wash them down. Fargo joined us for two large doggy biscuits and a couple of bites of pasta salad. Lobster, thank goodness, was not a favorite on his menu. His tastes were expensive enough.

Suddenly four mallards threw up a fine bow wave as they landed about fifteen feet off shore from us. They might well have been tame enough to swim in and waddle about hoping for tidbits. But the mighty Fargo dashed those hopes by running full tilt into the sea as if he meant to add all four to his dinner selection. They made hurried and awkward take-offs and flew away with disgruntled quacks, and Fargo splashed back, head held high with pride. Then, to show how clever he really was, he shook ice-cold water and sand all over both of us.

We both jumped up, brushing at the freezing water and grit. "Dammit, Fargo! Well, so much for gracious dining *al fresco*. How about a fire with our coffee? There's some driftwood scattered around."

"Perfect," Janet replied. "I'll just put the food back on ice."

I walked around picking up little branches of dry wood plus a couple of small logs. Suddenly, I straightened and swore. "Oh, hell and damnation! I left my cigarettes and lighter on the dashboard of the car."

Janet laughed. "You should see your face! I can't believe you forgot your cigarettes. Give me the keys. I'll go and get them. You look faint at the thought of those stairs."

She took off at a ground-covering jog, but by the time she returned, I had the fire laid and our coffee poured. I impressed her mightily by using the sandwich wrappers as the only paper needed to light the fire.

"Aren't you clever! If I must be shipwrecked, I'll make sure to take you along. You'd be invaluable in all sorts of interesting ways."

"Didn't the Coast Guard teach you survival techniques?"

"Minimal. I think those are more for Green Berets and other snake-eating types. Anyway, dummy, the Coast Guard doesn't get shipwrecked."

"You really liked it, didn't you? The Coast Guard."

"After the first couple of months, yes. I loved it—the structure and the belonging and security. I enjoyed even the hard work and I loved my times at sea. There was just enough danger from the weather, from a couple of rescue operations and from the few boats we stopped for a board-and-search, to give life an interesting edge. And I took close note of the officers—male and female—whom I admired. I tried to speak like them, act like them, dress like the women when they were in civilian clothes."

She reached out for a couple of little sticks and tossed them on the fire. "I was bound and determined to leave South Norwalk far, far behind me. And the CG was a good way to do it."

"The old role model routine. It's the way we all do it, I guess. I learned some things from my mom, some from Aunt Mae, a lot from some teachers I admired. Sounds like you could have done a lot worse for yourself, and that you were set for a long, happy cruise." Obviously something had gone wrong, but I waited, hoping she would tell me in her own time what it had been. Something told me it would be a mistake to ask.

"Yes, I figured I'd stay in the Coast Guard for eight years, not a twenty-year stint like my brother had planned for the army. I was saving almost everything I made, and although it wasn't a great deal at a time, it began to add up. I knew that when I got to the end of my enlistment I could count on the good old CG to pay for college. Then, with what I had and what I could borrow, I could get my restaurant. I'd still be barely thirty-two! And already I was changing from a scared little girl into a sure-footed adult with real focus. It was all taking shape."

Yes? Well? And? I asked silently. Then what? Obviously something went badly awry or else you'd still be in the Coast Guard, or off somewhere in college or running a restaurant. But no more information was forthcoming.

She seemed suddenly far away. Finally, after a lengthy silence, I sought to jump-start the conversation. "Did you stay in touch with your parents? Did you ever see them?" I asked, thinking maybe this was the problem.

"Once, early on. I went home on leave, so proud of my crisp uniform and its one little chevron. Mama kept patting me and telling me how grown up and important I looked. Then my father came home and announced that I looked like a dyke. My brothers and sister started the same garbage-talk they'd done with Eddie. It was *déjà vu* all over again. After that, like him, I just sent postcards."

Yeah, right from the edge, I thought. Talk about dysfunctional families—this one was a textbook classic. I tuned back in. I really hoped the whole day wouldn't be devoted to these modern day Jukes and Kallikacks. I wanted to know what had happened.

"Eventually," she went on almost dreamily, "I was transferred to Washington State. I had nearly six years in by then and a goodly collection of stripes on my sleeve and damn near twenty thousand dollars in the bank. I'd been to cook's school and loved it. Now, as I told you, I was in charge of the officer's club and mess outside Seattle."

More silence, more far-away looks. I'd had faster root canals. "Did you make the full eight years?" I didn't see how she could have. All along I had put her at about twenty-five, and that didn't quite add up. Say she went in at eighteen, and stayed in for eight years, she'd be a minimum of twenty-six, even if she'd just gotten out, and for some reason I didn't think she had. She just didn't seem like someone who'd been in uniform a short while ago. Had she been somewhere in college? Probably not, she had said she'd been working in Boston. Or, I belatedly wondered, had that story gone down the drain along with the family from New Hampshire?

She tossed the last drops of her coffee onto the sand and poured her now-empty cup full of wine, taking a healthy swig before answering me obliquely. "That's where I first met Terry, you know. In the Coast Guard."

"I had wondered about that," I replied neutrally.

"Yes. It was a good time for me." She suddenly became falsely vivacious, smiling and gesturing more broadly than was her habit, her voice tending to soar and swoop unnaturally. "She was from Connecticut, too, although nowhere near Norwalk. We had a wonderful time. We hit it off together from the moment we said hello. And as long as we were discreet on the base, we had no problem. Once off base in civvies, of course, we were free as birds. You'd *love* Seattle, Alex. We went to the Space Needle, of course, with that unbelievable view of the whole city and the harbor, and Pike's Market—why, there's absolutely *nothing* you can't buy there—from fresh fish and king crab and beautiful fresh vegetables to tee shirts and eighteen-karat gold jewelry!"

This was beginning to sound more like a guided tour of scenic Greater Seattle than an episode that must have ruined her career and damn near ruined her life. She seemed to have bad luck when it came to homophobia. Could she have run up against it again?

She poured more wine into her cup, sipped at it and rambled on. I half listened, leaning back lazily on the rumpled blanket, letting the words drift over me as she described landmark after landmark.

They had been to the art museum for a David Hockney retrospective. It was the first time she had seen a modern painter she actually thought she understood and maybe even liked. They had been to the Japanese Gardens and I would be *amazed* at the neatness and detail of every tiny area. Apparently tireless and endlessly curious, they had walked amid the gardens at the Chittenden Canal and watched pleasure boats go through the locks while sea lions played at their sides. They had gone to the zoo and seen a mother giraffe with . . .

All of a sudden the words simply floated unbidden from my lips. "Terry was Maynard Terrence O'Malley, wasn't he?"

# Chapter 12

Janet's head snapped up as if someone had suddenly pulled a string. "How . . . did . . . you . . . know?" Her voice was hoarse and horror-stricken, her eyes wide with shock and her fingers suddenly tight on the coffee mug.

"I'm not sure, really. A lot of little things began to add up, I guess—or not add up. Your reaction when I told you of finding the foot and when Sonny said the body had been found . . . it seemed somewhat of an over-reaction regarding some person you'd presumably never even heard of until then. Your not owning a car. I know lots of people in Boston who all have cars. They may not use them every day, but they own them."

My throat was dry. I cleared it noisily. "And then saying you didn't know what a Zodiac was, I guess that bothered me the most. I even dreamed about it. Then there were all those new clothes and no old ones. O'Malley's mother thinking he dated a girl named Jane

Peaches, although I must admit that was a stretch. And now Terry, not only in the Coast Guard, but also from Connecticut. It got to be too much. The penny finally dropped. Janet, sweetie, what on earth went on?"

"Yes. I can see how it would add up." Her voice was back to normal now—calm, somewhat impersonal, completely assured. "Well, my reactions to the finding of Terry's . . . body . . . were quite real, I assure you. The comment about the Zodiac was absolutely stupid. I realized that the minute I said it, but I was rattled. I'd been through a terrible experience, and you and Sonny can be just a wee bit intimidating, you know?"

She didn't sound intimidated now. Didn't she realize the trouble she was in? I really needed to talk to Sonny. This girl needed help, and fast.

"You and Sonny had me flustered. I even wondered if you had some reason for telling me these things, some suspicion of me, I should have said my car was in the body shop for repair or repo'd or something. Yes."

Her eyes twinkled, as if at some secret joke we shared. "But I never even gave the clothes a thought, if you can believe that. And I never knew about the Jane Peaches connection." She laughed outright. "Is that why you brought the peaches to the apartment this morning. As some sort of test? Was I supposed to press my hand to my heart and tell all when I saw them?"

I shook my head, annoyed. She could be so dead serious about something like the temperature of her wine, and now, in trouble up to her ears, she was being flip about an apparent involvement in a murder—two murders. Not only that, something much more personal was scaring me badly.

"Was Terry—or should I say Maynard?—your lover?" And did you use a condom, I desperately wanted to ask. Dear God, I hope she was careful!

"No. He was gay. Absolutely gay." I supposed I could believe that. I hoped so.

She gave a little moue of distaste. "But who in their right mind would want to be called Maynard? He used his middle name. We were never lovers, but good friends, Alex. Deep, true friends—I thought for life. Let me tell you what happened."

"I'd rather you didn't. No, I mean it." Janet had grinned and started to go on speaking. I overrode her. "Funny as you think it is, I *am* a private investigator and I hold a license from the State of Massachusetts. I am bound by law to report any crime I become aware of. And if you tell me what I think you're going to tell me, I have no choice but to head for the closest police station. Actually, I'm risking my license right now even if you don't say another word and all I do is take you home and drop you off and forget everything you've said." I knew I sounded pompous, but I didn't care. I meant it.

"Don't be silly, Alex, you're not about to lose your precious license. I promise, I won't tell you anything terrible that you will have to go haring home to Sonny about. It's just a simple explanation to clarify what happened." She reached out to pat my hand and I yanked it away as if I were dodging a wasp.

"Alex," she said gently, "Remember me? I am exactly the same person I was an hour ago."

"Maybe," I acknowledged grudgingly. "But I'm not. I can hardly overlook all this and then we just go merrily on like nothing happened."

"I told you yesterday—and you thought I was crazy—the one thing I cannot trust about you is your damned integrity! Now just relax for five minutes and let me give you a little totally innocent, uncompromising background. You'll see how little I really was involved in all this. Trust me."

I gave her a sour look, but nodded slightly. This time it was I who poured some wine and swallowed deeply. I knew we should have brought both bottles or maybe a case. I wanted so badly to believe her. After all, she'd been a kid when she joined up, and God knows her parents had never been a stabilizing influence. She hadn't had a chance to build up many internal resources. It would have been easy for her to make mistakes. I turned back to what she was saying.

"One evening Terry came over to me in the Petty Officers' Club. I figured it was the opening gambit of a hit, but then he said he was from Connecticut and had heard I was, too. And I had learned it was possible to be homesick for a place you'd never liked and never wanted to see again. So I answered pleasantly enough." She took a deep breath, as if to gather strength.

"Well, we chatted about various towns and places we both knew, for nearly an hour. A few days later he called, saying that since we were so near Seattle, it seemed a shame not to explore it and would I like to go in for the day? I still figured him for straight and hoped I wasn't setting us both up for an unhappy scene, but I liked him, and I liked the idea of a trip into Seattle, so I agreed. Of course it didn't take long for each of us to discover the other was gay."

"How very convenient for you," I remarked dryly. She ignored me and rushed on.

"From then on, we had the best of both worlds. Our fellow Coast Guardsmen thought we were dating each other. We had lots of fun together and each of us could have the occasional fling of our choice with no one the wiser. Life was good. I wasn't saving quite as much money as I had been, but at last I was having some fun and feeling like a human being again."

"Where are you going with this, Janet? On another tour of Seattle?"

She continued to ignore me and rattled on as if she were racing against some sort of time fuse. "As we got to know each other, I learned that Terry's life was very different from mine, and yet very similar. His family in Stonington had been comfortable, as he put it—I would have said rich. Terry had gone to private school and then to Yale. Toward the end of his junior year, his father had a fatal heart attack. When the dust settled, it came to light that the family had 'lived-up' to most of the money Terry's father had made, and very little had been put aside. After all, he hadn't expected to die so young."

She gave an almost Gallic shrug. "An uncle helped his mother get settled comfortably. But nothing would be left to pay for Terry's final year at Yale. The uncle refused to pay it, although Terry said the man could have easily afforded it. The miserable crab told Terry he should get a student loan, sell his sports car and get some kind of job. Poor Terry would have had to face all his wealthy friends, resign from his clubs and work as a waiter or something."

Well, gol-ll-ly gee! Poor little boy! I thought what three years at Yale would have meant to me or Sonny, and I couldn't come up with a single sympathetic grunt.

But the monologue wasn't over. "His family had let him down so badly he just couldn't handle it. He said he felt completely abandoned, so he quit Yale and got good and drunk one night. He met some Coasties in a bar who convinced him he could have a great time in the Coast Guard, and the next day he joined up. Still a little drunk, he said."

"He sounds like a spoiled brat to me."

"Alex, don't you understand? He had *counted* on his family and they let him down! As Terry said, his father picked a most inopportune time to die."

"Kind of like my father grabbed an electric line so Sonny and I would have to get summer jobs to help Mom out?"

"Well," she bristled defensively, "It's not all that different, is it, really? And like Papa saying out of the blue that once I graduated high school I had to pay room and board. Never mind I needed the money for college."

"So what? Now you had assured tuition for college from the CG," I pointed out.

"Yeah, but that didn't quite work out."

"Did you get a nasty commanding officer or something? Were you going to be transferred to the Dry Tortugas? What could have been bad enough to make you quit the Coasties?"

"I didn't exactly quit. There was a little mix-up with some of Seattle's finest."

Cops! My God what had Terry gotten her into? I tried to sound casual. Hah. "In the wrong place at the wrong time?"

She lit one of my cigarettes and blew the smoke out dramatically. "Was I ever! And it all started so innocently . . . as a wonderful celebration." Gazing sadly across the water, she looked like a waif from Jane Eyre's orphanage. I didn't know whether to be hopping mad or lovingly empathetic. But I knew we had to straighten this out. "Stop stalling Janet. What happened?"

"Well, you know how badly I want my restaurant. Terry told me he wanted a bookstore just as badly. One night sitting in our favorite bar, we realized what fun it would be to combine the two. We were just thrilled at the idea! And I do think it's a great one, still. Terry wanted to celebrate with champagne and a big Alaska crab dinner, but it was near payday and we were both broke."

"So you walked out on a tab?" Could pulling teeth be this hard? No. There would be no dentists.

"Oh, no. We would never do that. There was a nearby liquor store where Terry said he had spent loads of money. He said the old lady who ran it kind of liked him. He was sure she would lend him seventy-five dollars so we could have our dinner."

"That sounds pretty unreal."

"It did to me, too, Alex. But Terry could be unbelievably persuasive. So I walked over with him. To give him a little privacy, I moved toward the back and pretended to be shopping for wine. The next thing I knew, I heard the woman laugh and say something in a nasty tone. I looked up just in time to see Terry pop her on the jaw and scoop money out of the till. He screamed, 'Run, Janet, run!' And we both ran back to the bar."

Her eyes were focused on a distant point, recalling the scene. "We got back to the bar. I was terrified, but Terry seemed sort of on a high. He gave the bartender a hundred to say we never left. He ordered a split of champagne, but I couldn't even drink that. I couldn't believe what he had done. And of course, when the old woman and the police arrived, they didn't believe the bartender—or us—and took us in."

"My God, Janet! Terry committed assault and robbery and you were with him! Did you get a lawyer?"

"Umm. Finally. A little pipsqueak lieutenant, J.G. from the base, who just got into a lengthy, silly pissing contest with the cops over jurisdiction. Finally, I said I was exhausted from answering all the questions and could I go. The J.G. woke up and asked if the cops had continued to question us after we'd requested a lawyer. We said, yes, and we were out. The cops broke the law."

"Janet, did you have any idea Terry was going to strike and rob that woman?"

"No, and to be honest, Alex, I don't think he did either. But she not only refused, she laughed at him and said something about his being a 'kept pretty boy,' and he just couldn't take anymore."

"Couldn't take anymore!" I exploded. "He was the one who started it all! You were as innocent as the woman he hit. Why didn't you tell anyone?" Well, it still wasn't too late. We could get this cleared up. Chief Wood would know what to do.

"I told the cops. They didn't care. I told the J.G. He was too busy congratulating himself for getting us out. My commander agreed with you. She said if I swore an affidavit to everything that really happened, I'd probably just get a CG letter of reprimand in my personnel jacket and that would be it. It might slow down my promotion a few months, but no more. But that would have meant squealing on Terry. I couldn't do that. He was a friend. You do not let friends down."

I could have shaken her until *she* squealed. "Janet, ratting on a school chum over who was smoking in the locker room is not the same as ruining a career over a self-centered, greedy, vicious, spoiled brat. Especially over an incident in which you played no active part."

She sat with her knees pulled up under her chin, arms wrapped tightly around them, as if she might fly apart if she didn't hold

138

herself fast. "I don't really disagree with you at this point. But at that time, Alex, I really cared for Terry. He was intense, fun. He was . . . *classy*. He was my friend . . . *my friend*. He was in trouble. I couldn't do it. Surely you can understand that. Just as you must see that I did nothing wrong."

Terry had been the Pied Piper to her. I understood that. I remembered a boy in my high school who was much the same. He convinced me and a few friends we were somehow above everyone else. And what fun we had—riding in his convertible, cutting class, sassing teachers, drinking beer and smoking pot he'd paid for. I damn near followed him right down the primrose path.

But I had family who cared, a very special teacher who wouldn't let go and maybe a bit of the good sense that I'd absorbed from my mother and Aunt Mae. Things Janet had not had. If the little two-bit tootler I'd known had come so close to snaring me, what must Terry have done to Janet with his talk of Yale and country clubs and sports cars, his perfect speech and manners, the self-assurance of growing up with money? She never stood a chance.

I sighed. "I understand you blew a career and a future that meant the world to you over this slug. What was the outcome?"

She looked blankly into the cup of wine as if a suitable answer would miraculously float to the surface. Then she looked up at me as if her heart were broken. I could see tears welling up in her eyes. When she spoke, her voice was flat, as if any sound of emotion would make the wound bleed fatally. "We resigned 'for the good of the service.' They discharged us where we had enlisted. So there I was back in Connecticut with only the money I had scrimped and saved for my restaurant, knowing it would never be enough, that I would never have my dream."

She drank some wine and continued. "Terry and I stood in the rain at the train station in New London, tickets to Stamford in our hands. We were back. Worse than when we started."

I took her hands in mine. They were icy. "Janet, I know you've been through hell. Let me help. We'll talk to Sonny and Chief Wood—get some people working for you for a change."

She shook her head. "It won't work, Alex." She sounded hopeless. "There's been too much."

Too much. No, no there hadn't been too much else. This situation had to be salvageable. She was one hundred percent innocent in the Seattle mess. That bastard Terry had indeed put her in the wrong place at the wrong time. That was all. And she'd had no one around strong enough to make her take care of herself. Well, I would damn well see to it!

It was vital to get it on record that she had been only present, or even a frightened, unwilling small accomplice, in the robberies. I had a sudden vision of her, in jeans and sweater, wearing a watch cap, sporting dark makeup and a little mustache. I bet she was cute as hell, like a little girl dressed up for Halloween. And then she cocked her tiny forefinger and thumb and lisped, "Give me all your money, and please give me a Milky Way, too. Bang, bang. You're dead."

But I had no time for those thoughts. The old man . . . no, it had to have been Terry who killed him. Assume she had shot Terry, it had to have been in self-defense. We had to get the facts in order, and as non-threatening as possible, before she was charged. And get her a good lawyer. That was paramount.

I squeezed her hands and pulled her to her feet. "Darling, you've got to trust me in this. It is not too late. The first thing we must do is get to Sonny, so you can explain this whole . . ."

"No, Alex, no cops. Even Sonny would never understand all this. He's nice, but he is a cop, and I saw them in Seattle and how they reacted to us. They didn't want to hear what really happened or why. They just wanted to put us in jail. No cops, no jail for me. I don't deserve that and I will not have it!" She looked at me almost smugly.

"Then a lawyer," I countered. "I know a bright guy in Provincetown. He can at least make sure you don't make any mistakes until you can get a criminal guru over from Boston."

"You still don't understand, do you, Alex? I'm not about to turn myself in to anyone. Maybe you trust the law to protect me, but I don't! I haven't done anything really wrong. I've told you it was all Terry. All! I'm going back to Seattle and live my life."

She spun on her toes and sprinted down the beach. I stood, dumbstruck for a moment, and then ran after her. I had gotten a slow start, not realizing she was actually running away. She ran like a deer and I did not. My legs were longer, but I was barefoot—and heavier—and—hell, older. As I ran, I cursed every cigarette and donut I'd ever seen. I was falling rapidly behind. Fargo loped easily at my side, grinning and occasionally looking up at me with a gleeful glint in his eye. I knew what he was thinking: usually he ran and I walked. Now for some reason I was running with him. Ain't we got fun!

By the time I reached the foot of the steps, Janet had scampered up them and was out of sight. Now I could only hope that maybe some total stranger had stolen my car while we were picnicking, or that my car battery would pick today for its expiration date or—the only realistic possibility—that Janet would misgauge the narrow turnaround and get the car stuck in the sand. When I reached the top of the endless stairway, my vision was blurred and my breathing sounded like an old steam locomotive idling in some deserted seaside station. Neither Janet nor the car was anywhere within sight.

I sank to my knees and tried to get my breath back. I thought of all the stuff left on the beach. Should I go back and get it? No. That would take too much time, and I wasn't sure I would ever make it up those steps again. Most importantly, I had to stop Janet somehow. She was so frightened she was completely over the edge. She was fixated on Seattle and that double-damned restaurant as her sole salvation. If she could get to the one and open the other, then—in her mind—none of this God-awful mess would have ever happened.

I wondered where on earth I had been for the last week. Janet had thrown out warning signs like she was sowing grass seed. Obviously Sonny had had his doubts long before I did. Of course he hadn't been looking at her brown eyes as an invitation to incredible delight, either. He hadn't enjoyed the midnight giggles, or the first-light drowsy passion, or the shower-fresh smell of her hair. He would not be standing here, astonished and horrified that Janet was now truly a fugitive, going as fast as my car would carry her, into ever-deepening trouble. She had to be stopped. And I, as Dad used to say, was a day late and a dollar short.

Unfortunately, I was afraid she'd be so intent upon escape she'd drive the car into a bridge or a tree, or if some Nervous Nelly cop stopped her, she'd take a swing at him and get herself shot in the process. A phone was my first priority. I started walking as fast as I could down the road.

Within fifty feet I wished I'd gone back for my shoes. Within a hundred I was limping and muttering "ooh, ooh, ooh" and wincing with every step. At last, a house. I walked up to the door and knocked. A woman peered out a front window and yelled, "Go away! Get out of here or I'll call the cops." I wondered if she were some sort of hermit, or had some unreasonable fear of visitors.

"Do that!" I shouted back. "Please do so at once!" I limped on. I came to a house with several rental cottages grouped around it. And all still padlocked for the winter. Down the road a blue van approached. Two adults were in the front, two children in the back. My God, it had Jersey plates! It was the one I had seen on the beach the day I found Terry's foot! I began frantically to flag them down. Surely they would recognize Fargo and me. Quite possibly they would even have a cell phone.

"Hey! Hey! It's me! I saw you on the beach last week. Hey! I need some help!" Just before they reached me they turned into a driveway, then backed out and raced back down the road the way they had come. I couldn't believe they hadn't recognized me, especially with Fargo beside me. What was wrong with everyone? Onward, slowly and ever so painfully onward.

Finally, there was a house with signs of life around it. A car sat in the drive and lawn furniture was piled haphazardly in the yard. I knocked, the door opened and immediately slammed in my face. As

I began to call out and knock again, I heard a woman's voice through an open window, apparently on the phone. "A regular wild woman, with a slavering big black dog. Hurry, she's pounding on my door, looks like a maniac, crazy as a loon. Probably as soon kill me as not! Hurry!"

I backed away from the door and took stock. Barefoot, limping and groaning, probably beet red, windblown, pouring sweat, shirt-tail flapping—I may not have been at my personal best, and Fargo *was* slavering a bit. I'm sure he was thirsty. Oh, maybe the people in the van *had* recognized us.

I shuffled away from the door and down the driveway to sit on a rock and await the Truro police I was sure were on the way. I lit a cigarette. Why not? It was too late now. And I thought how clever it was of me to have the cigarettes and lighter handily tucked in my shirt pocket, while my cell phone was in the compartment of my car, on its way to Seattle!

I wanted them to hurry, certainly as much as the distraught woman did. There were only two bridges leading off of Cape Cod to the mainland and the various Interstate highways. If the State Police could block both bridges before Janet could reach one of them, there was no question of her escape. The only other way off the Cape was by water and I couldn't believe she could manage to steal another boat, this one in broad daylight. It was about a sixty-mile drive from where we were to the bridges. Janet had about a twenty-minute start, and these things did not take place in real life as quickly as they seemed to on television.

I was happy to hear a siren howling in the distance.

Unfortunately, I didn't know either cop. One of them listened to my disjointed tale with a blank, polite face, while the other asked the homeowner endlessly if she were all right, if I had threatened or molested her in any way—not that I could think why anyone would.

At last, they decided I should accompany them back to the police station for further discussion, toward which they drove at an infuri-atingly sedate pace. Fargo and I were in the back seat. He kept licking at the driver's neck, while I leaned forward to hector the other officer unsuccessfully about radioing ahead for a roadblock. None of us was happy by the time we reached the station.

The senior officer at the police station had gone to school with Sonny, so things brightened at once. Fargo got a drink. I got a soda. Phone calls were made to the State Police. And our original driver provided Fargo and me with an ungracious lift to the Provincetown Police Station. There, Mitch took one look at me and shoved me into Sonny's office out of sight, so I wouldn't frighten any small children, visitors or prisoners, I guess.

Mitch reminded me that Sonny had driven down to Connecticut earlier that day with the purpose of interviewing O'Malley's mother. He thought she might know more than she realized and hoped a friendly little chat might reveal something valuable. He was also going to see the Connecticut state cops and see if there was any way he could speed up an ID on the robbers' car. Sonny had told me all this earlier that morning, but it seemed now like news from a lifetime ago.

As I nodded tiredly Mitch added, "The state police are cooperating regarding closing the bridges, but with all the time that passed, it'll be a close run thing."

"Yeah. But I tried, Mitch, I really did. That damn Truro cop just wouldn't . . ."

"No, no. I didn't mean you were at fault, Alex, not at all. But have you any idea where she is?"

"Route Six, I guess. Oh, I see what you mean." My brain moved slowly. "Maybe Boston. She had an apartment—no, I guess she didn't. Forget it. I can't think of anything helpful."

Mitch looked at me with concern. "No problem, Alex. Just take it easy. And if you're okay to drive, take my car down and collect your stuff off the beach. One way or another it won't be there very long. And don't worry about the car, I won't need it till tomorrow late."

What an angel! One less detail to worry about. Fargo curled up on the front seat and immediately went to sleep. At that point I realized how tired I was and concentrated on my driving. It had been a long and draining day, begun with such bright promise and now coming to an end with—quite literally—heavy clouds, as the predicted cold front moved in.

I wondered if Janet had been caught. If not, what would she do? The gas tank of my car was almost full, but I doubted she had a great deal of money with her. And credit cards, if she had them, would leave a dangerous trail. I parked the car and trudged down the beach, Fargo walking close by my side, too tired to bother with any sideline adventures.

As we went along, I noticed that the surf was building on a grey and sullen sea, and the tide was coming in. When we reached the little cove, I was surprised to see the cooler now resting safely above the high tide mark with the blanket folded compactly on its lid. My sneakers and socks were placed neatly inside the cooler, weighting it against the rising wind. All the leftover food and drinks were gone, however, probably to a teenage picnic around the next curve in the beach. In my fatigue, my immediate thought was to contact the Chamber of Commerce with a new slogan: *Visit Cape Cod, Where Even Thieves Have A Heart*.

I laughed and the tears began. I sat down in the sand and donned shoes and socks and cried aloud, like a child. Fargo came and sat very straight and very still beside me, leaning close against my shoulder. I rested my cheek on his broad, silky head and felt immeasurably comforted.

# Chapter 13

I pulled Mitch's car into my driveway, relieved not to have to think about returning it right now. Waiting for the garage door to rumble up and putting the car back in gear to drive in seemed a terrible effort. I could not remember being so weary, so drained. I let Fargo out. I went to the utility room in the back of the garage, where I rinsed out the cooler and tossed the blanket on top of the washer for later.

I seemed able to focus only on one simple thing at a time. Lock the car. Close the little garage side door. My body was screaming for rest and my mind was definitely on some sort of overload. Maybe that's how Janet felt. But it was probably a very bad idea to think of Janet right now.

As Fargo and I walked toward the house, the wind felt gusty, and it held little spurts of rain that hit my face and jacket like cool playful slaps. The rain felt good at that moment, but there'd probably be nothing playful about it later. The wind was increasing and veering to the north. I guessed our cold front was here.

Inside, I fed and watered the dog and thought longingly about a drink for myself. But I felt somehow both sweaty and chilled, with a heavy, raspy undercoat of sand. Better to make it first the shower, then the drink.

Some minutes later I came back into the kitchen feeling a little more human, clad in warm pajamas and soft—very soft—slippers. I looked at Fargo and was envious. He had eaten most of his food, had some water and was sound asleep in his bed. He was neither upset about today nor worried about tomorrow. He was fed, warm, safe and on the side of the angels. I almost woke him up just to have some company, but I didn't have the heart.

Instead, I made a bourbon and water and took it into the living room where I could relax and prop up my sore feet on the coffee table. Mitch had assured me he would call at once if there was any news about Janet or from Sonny. I noticed that my phone message indicator was blinking to me that I had one call. I jumped to my feet, ignoring the soreness, and reached eagerly for the playback button. Janet, let it be Janet. Please.

It was Sonny. "Hi. It's Sunday about ten a.m. I stopped by the office on my way out, and this was on my voice mail. I thought you would be interested. I won't be back till late tonight or tomorrow, so I'll let you hear it now. See you later."

After a series of bells and whistles a man's voice came over the speaker. It sounded sort of defeated. "Sonny? This is Bob Reynolds, Plymouth Police. Don't ever even mention anything Irish to me again. The travel agent went and told Mrs. McKinney I was asking about them and they called my chief. He called me in and reamed me a new one. It seems he's good friends with them. The chief and his wife went on that Wales tour and also on the London tour. Apparently everybody on the tour knew they were taking the ferry from Wales to Ireland, because Mrs. McKinney's grandmother was going to be ninety or a hundred, and there was some big family reunion with relatives from all over."

There was a slight pause, more static, throat-clearing. I had the distinct feeling that Officer Reynolds would like to cry. Well, sorry, Bob, that's the kind of day it's been. The tape rolled on.

"The chief and his wife went on the London tour with Mrs. McKinney a couple of years later, and she left early because she got a wire her grandmother had upped and died on them. So she went to the funeral in Ireland. Sonny, they are upright citizens. They never even heard about the IRA. They wouldn't know a criminal if they saw one. They have never loaned their boat to no one, much less to carry guns. The chief told me if I saw them driving down the street with a cannon tied to the back of their car, I was to assume they were going to a Fourth of July celebration, even if it was February. And I will be working the midnight to eight a.m. shift for the rest of my life."

I heard a brief burst of Sonny's laughter, a click, then silence. I had to smile, even as my heart went out to the poor man. All his troubles for nothing! I didn't need the tape to tell me the great IRA caper had been a fantasy with its outline cleverly sketched by Janet, and the colors all foolishly filled in by the rest of us.

I thought of calling Mitch, but there was no point in bothering him. He would call whenever something happened.

And when would that be? And what would it be? Tired as I was, I still felt edgy. I wanted this situation resolved, and there was not one single thing I could do to make that happen. I don't deal well in that position. Unfortunately for my peace of mind and sometimes for the outcome of events, I am of the do-something-even-if-it's-wrong school. But even I couldn't think of anything to do tonight.

The house was dead quiet. It seemed strangely empty. I had been getting used to having Janet around, or about to be around, or on the phone. I guessed I'd better get un-used to it. The old C&W song . . . alone again . . . naturally.

I thought back to the afternoon. Had Janet taken my car keys by intent or accident? She would have taken the cigarettes and lighter from the dashboard, then locked the car and automatically have put the keys in her pocket for the walk back to our spot on the beach. She probably merely forgot to return them, just as I forgot to ask for them. Then, when she panicked at the thought of police and lawyers, she simply had them, ready to use.

I wondered where Janet was on this cold, unwelcoming night. Still driving, hastening through the darkness, fearing every set of headlights that appeared behind her? Holed up somewhere in a motel for the night, waiting for the heavy knock upon the door? In jail, wondering if she would ever be free? In a hospital, hurt and alone? Wrapped around a tree in the fatal steel embrace of my car? None of my scenarios were happy ones.

And I can tell you that it is a very difficult exercise in mental calisthenics suddenly to categorize your lover as quite possibly a killer, a murderer. You think of butterfly kisses and soft caresses. You see warm laughter playing around the lips and in the eyes. You remember shared showers and fast, hard hugs. You recall the silly banter and the serious conversations. You recollect again and again how she said she loved you—and you believe that—but you also wonder how she would have felt about you if you'd owned a liquor store in Plymouth.

The phone rang and I jumped about a foot. It was Mitch. Janet had apparently beaten the roadblocks at the bridges. No car matching mine had tried to cross. There was no report of anyone seeing my car anywhere along Route Six. They were now checking secondary roads. A multi-state alarm was now out for the car, he informed me. Great. I had visions of what shape it would be in when—if—I ever got it back.

Continuing his update, Mitch added that Sonny had called. He was in Stamford, Connecticut and gathering some interesting information, but would go into details upon his return tomorrow. He was sorry about my car and about Janet, of course. Of course. Looking back, I thought Sonny had been suspicious of her for a while now. I realized that I had been, too, but my suspicions had floated just below the surface of my conscious thought. I'd been too busy teetering along the edge of love to let them come into my waking thoughts.

Naively, I had insisted on pursuing the gun-running possibility because that's what I had wanted to believe. I wished to God I had listened to my brain instead of my hormones. Do some people actually do that?

I had another drink and a TV mystery dinner while I watched a nice impersonal account of the Mexican War of the 1840s on The History Channel. I actually became interested in how many future Civil War generals had learned their trade as junior officers in that conflict. Then I must have dozed, for when I opened my eyes, German Messerschmidts were diving across the sky, and I didn't think they had been around in the 19th century. It must be time for bed.

So I let the dog out, and right back in. Fargo will happily swim in 38-degree water, but the first drop of rain sends him scurrying for his bed. We retired shortly. I was sapped and stiff and depressed. Then and there I resolved to cut the smoking all together, drink only spring water and eat nothing but plain yogurt and crabgrass for the rest of my life. My performance that afternoon had been pitiful.

Surprisingly, I fell fast asleep on those happy thoughts and slumbered late and soundly until Fargo woke me the next morning with a rather desperate look in his eye.

A cold but bright, sunny day revealed itself, flashing little coded messages on the leftover raindrops on the grass. A mug of hot strong coffee helped both my attitude and my ambition. I lifted the phone off its wall cradle and began to make a series of calls. I was not looking forward to any of them.

First of course, was to the police station, where I was startled to hear Mitch answer. "God, Mitch, don't they let you go home and sleep at night?" I asked.

"Not these days," he sighed. "We're really short of people. Sonny's away. Palmer's out with a broken ankle. Sanchez is in some little village in Portugal looking up his ancestors, and the chief is over at Mass General with his wife—she's got some sort of heart problem. Serious, I think."

"I didn't even know Pauline was ill. I'm sorry to hear that. She's such a nice woman. I'll have to call her when she gets home. Isn't Captain Anders there somewhere? He should be *some* help."

"Yeah, he's here. Buried under the Wall Street Journal, Barron's and Investor's Daily and stuck on the phone to his broker. Seems the stock market opened today with a resounding fart."

I laughed. "Couldn't happen to a nicer guy. I take it there's no news? I mean news for us."

"Nary a word anywhere. Sorry."

"Yeah. Well, I'll drop your car off after lunch if that's okay."

"No rush, Alex." He added morosely, "Keep it as long as you need. Believe me, by the time I get out of here, it'll be time to trade the car."

We hung up and I moved on to call number two, this time Aunt Mae. Janet would not be going to the Herb Center with her this afternoon. It was not an easy call. Naturally, I had to give her a brief recap of all that had happened. She was sympathetic but not gushy, thank God, and even offered to call my mother, "before she hears it on the news or from someone in town, dear. We can't have her learning it second hand, you know. She'd be terribly worried about you."

I was grateful, for the offer—it would be one less difficult call—and for her parting words. "I know you must be terribly disappointed and unhappy, my dear child, but you must try not to feel any guilt. You have only been present at the end of this sad tale. You were not involved in any of the events that led up to it. Remember that."

I would try, I promised. Aunt Mae's advice was always sage and to the point. I wondered if she'd consider giving me a weekly appointment. God knows I could use it, and at least we'd keep the money in the family.

One more call. This one to Larry Cole, my insurance agent, whose attitude would lead you to believe every claim was paid for out of his own pocket, denying food to his hungry wife and kinder. When I was put through to him, I decided to try and keep it simple and brief. "Larry, I just wanted to let you know, my car's been stolen. Yesterday about four in the afternoon, over on the beach turn-around down past the Truro lighthouse."

"Oh, hell. Do the police know?"

"Absolutely."

"Well, that's a right move anyway. They'll be on the lookout. Where did you report it? Provincetown? Or just Truro?"

"They both know. So do the State Police."

"Oh, good thinking. Probably just teenagers joyriding. It'll turn up soon. At least I hope so, maybe even undamaged." Larry looked at every dollar as if it were the last one he would ever see. "No idea who it was, of course?"

"Yes, it was a friend of mine named Janet Meacham."

"Some friend! How did she get in it? Wasn't it locked? Where do you think she went? How do you know it was her—she?"

"She had the keys. I had given them to her earlier to get something from the car. She hadn't given them back when she decided to leave. She just drove off. And I can assure you I wish I did know where!"

"Oh, well now, Alex, this doesn't sound like a theft we'd necessarily be responsible for. I imagine she just kind of borrowed the car." He sounded relieved. "Not that she shouldn't have asked you, of course," he added quickly, "but I'll bet she brings it back any minute and good as new!" He would consider it good as new if two doors and the steering wheel were missing.

"Larry, I say again, it is stolen. The police in about ten states are looking for it. The young woman is wanted for questioning in a double murder."

There was a long silence. "Stay in touch, Alex. Let me know when it—ah, turns up." He did not say goodbye.

I graduated to a beer and lit my third cigarette. Well, at least I was still counting them. Anyway, I was under a lot of stress. This was no time to add to it by trying to break a habit. And beer had various nutrients, I had read. I still planned to improve and purify my lifestyle, but today was not cut out for harping on minor health issues, I reassured myself.

Suddenly, for some reason I wondered if Terry smoked. Probably, with a long holder like Franklin Roosevelt. He sounded effete. I did not like Terry. I actively disliked Terry. I realized I was not in the least sorry he was dead, told myself I should feel guilty—and didn't. He'd had everything handed to him, and the first ripple in his life had tossed him on his ass.

I wondered why he'd joined the Coast Guard? Probably the two Coasties he'd met in the bar were gay and told him how easy it was to pick up guys when you were good looking and wore a uniform, I thought sourly.

Terry was everything Janet longed to be. Sophisticated, Ivy League, suave, clever, self-confident on the surface and—at least at one time—rich. Had she only realized it, she was worth ten of him. I was morally certain that if someone had sent Janet to Yale for three years and then told her she'd have to handle the fourth pretty much on her own, she'd have graduated if she'd had to earn money cleaning the men's room at the local bus station.

It was strange. Terry had a head start on life that most people would have envied. And he couldn't handle one setback. Janet had overcome a number of fairly serious adversities. She had even managed to save $20,000 on a CG salary, which couldn't have left much for fun or life's little luxuries. Her life was finally moving smoothly toward what she wanted most—that damned restaurant— and she blew it over some naive idea that the kind of upper class person she wanted to become wouldn't rat on a friend. And it wouldn't even have been ratting. All she had to do was disassociate herself from an incident that was all Terry's fault in the first place.

All that, of course, assumed that it was true. And I had discovered lately that with Janet, that assumption was not automatic. No family in New Hampshire. No girl Terry. No Boston job or apartment. I had thought I was getting to know her so well. Now I wondered who Janet was. And how many Janets there were.

Much as I hated to think it, Janet's school counselor—homophobic or no—had been right on the button.

I got up to take another beer from the fridge and the phone rang. I spun to grab it, tripped over the dog, and went down in a heap, swearing. I finally disentangled myself, heaved to my feet and lunged for the phone. "Yeah?"

"Darling! You're panting. Have you been jogging or something?"

"And hello to you, too, Mom." Was the entire world trying to improve my physical condition? "No, I was not jogging. I fell over the dog."

"Oh, goodness. Is he all right?"

I heard him jump onto the living room couch. "I assume so. He has retired to the couch to recover. I'm all right, too, mother. Thanks for asking."

"I'm glad, dear, don't be grumpy. I'm sorry about your car and your friend. I just wanted to tell you . . . I have to go to work this afternoon, but I'd be glad to run you up to Hyannis to pick up a rental tomorrow. And if you need a car today we can work something out with mine."

"Oh, thanks, Mom, that would be great. I have Mitch's car for today, but tomorrow it would be really helpful to get a rental."

"Okay, then I'll see you around ten in the morning. And, Alex, your Aunt Mae filled me in on a little background here, so I know it must be extremely upsetting to find that Janet is involved in this situation. But thank God it came to light now rather than sometime in the future. Later it might well have affected your life much more deeply, in more ways than one."

"I know, Mom. I thought of that. See you in the morning. Thanks." I felt my eyes begin to burn, and I reflected briefly that I was lucky in my family. They did not judge my personal or professional life, they were there when I needed them, and they loved me.

You couldn't ask for a whole lot more. I compared them to Janet's un-lovely bevy of relatives and wondered how different her life might have been if she'd had my family. One part of me insisted there would have been a 180-degree difference. But another small, sad inner voice told me Janet's life would probably have ended in some sort of disaster no matter who she called Mom.

I shoved the chair back with a determined scrape and stood up. "Come on, Fargo. You going to sleep all day? You know you promised to take me to the beach!" On the way to the back door I grabbed my camera, jacket and his leash. I tried hard to pretend it was just another day, but I found no film-worthy scenes at Race Point. The sun-filled day and deep blue water held no charms. Fargo's antics produced no laughter. A couple walking with arms entwined did not soften my heart. I was nervous and irritable. Obviously, when I felt like this, only one thing would help: food. It was nearly two o'clock, and I'd had nothing to eat since my small, low fat, though gourmet (well, the label *said* it was) TV dinner the night before.

I decided to return Mitch's car before I ate. I really hated to keep it any longer, even if he didn't actually need it. On the way to the police station I filled the tank and picked up a six-pack of his favorite brew, which I stashed behind the passenger seat, out of sight. I put Fargo on his lead and we went inside to learn that Sonny had not yet been seen and nothing had been heard of Janet.

"Any idea at *all* where she might be?" Mitch pocketed his keys. "Could she have had friends somewhere up-Cape?"

"She's somewhere between here and Seattle. That's all I know. I have no idea about any friends or where they might be. Maybe Chatham, she said she was stationed there. And as I said, maybe Norwalk, Connecticut. I don't even want to think about it, Mitch. I can't make sense of anything about this whole situation. Thanks for the car. Look on the floor when you get in." I winked at him.

"Oh? Oh. You didn't need to do that, but thanks."

"My pleasure. Anything new from Himself?"

"Not since this morning, and I can't say I'm sorry. I'm gonna be high on his shit list."

"Why, Mitch!" I laughed. "You? What did you do, make a coffee ring on his blotter?"

"You can laugh. He's not *your* sergeant. No, as soon as he heard about Janet running yesterday, he told me to search Janet's place, to see if she left a gun, money, any information where she went. You know, the usual. And he said put up some crime scene tape. Anything there was now evidence."

He looked very uncomfortable. "Don't tell me you found another foot?" I asked. One small part of me wasn't laughing.

"We found nothing. Jeanine and I got there right after Mrs. M. got home from evening church. The Sunday lesson must have been on criminal law. I asked Mrs. M. for a key, told her what we wanted to do and why and stood there smiling, with my hand out like a fool. The next words out of her mouth were, 'Do you have a warrant?'"

"Oh, no."

"Yep. I told her she could give us permission to go in. She said no way. She had rented it to Janet and only *she* could give us permission to search. She added—you know, she began to sound like a defense lawyer. She added that as far as she knew, no crime had been committed there and no one was inside in danger. So, no warrant, no key. And Mrs. M.—Mrs. *Madeiros*—shut the door in my face."

He shook his head, still in disbelief. "And this morning, we've been so short-handed, I haven't had anybody to start chasing down a judge. I'll do it when I can. The hell with Sonny. What'd he find so damn interesting in Connecticut, anyway?"

"Tell 'em, tiger!"

Fargo and I walked up to the Wharf Rat Bar, where I tethered him to the big anchor and went inside. The usual suspects were gathered at their back table. They became silent as I entered, which told me they'd been talking about me—or Janet—or Sonny—or Terry before I came in.

I waved and called out, "Carry on, gentlemen, don't let me interrupt."

I stopped at the bar, where Joe produced a Bud and his usual sour grin. "You interrupted, all right. They are about evenly divided as to whether you gave the girl your car so she could escape and meet you somewhere later, or she stole the car and has run off to meet Sonny, wherever he is. Harmon defends you both. He says you gave the girl your car, but that Sonny was waiting, hiding down the road to follow her into New York City, knowing she will lead him to the drug king-pin who is behind the whole thing."

"Jesus. You know, I could make millions as Harmon's agent. Every sentence he utters could be the plot for a made-for-TV movie."

"Honey, doncha know it! Now, I figure she got your car away from you somehow. What did she do, pull a gun on you?"

"Nothing so dramatic." I told him more or less the truth. "We were on the beach. I gave her the keys to get something out of my car, which made it real simple for her. She just plain drove away. And she's a young woman, Joe, not a girl."

"Yeah, whatever. She kill that guy who came up caught in *Ocean Pearl's* net? And that old guy in the store over in Plymouth?"

"Nobody's sure of anything." I felt sick, hearing the words so casually uttered. No doubt Joe was secretly celebrating his good luck in striking out with Janet.

"They just want to talk to her. Joe, I need food." I sipped my beer till Joe got back with my lunch, and mused on how information seemed simply to percolate through Provincetown. You never even heard a jungle drum. Something happened and everybody in town knew about it, inaccurately usually, but with incredible speed. Finally, Joe arrived bearing a pastrami sandwich with French fries and a big slice of half-sour pickle. I figured it was a health-food lunch: meat, grain, vegetable and a little something green.

I took the last hefty bite of the sandwich outside to Fargo and we started for home. Today I hadn't felt easy, even in the Rat. Ordinarily the Rat's regulars amused and amazed me, and actually, I rather liked them. Today their half-concealed winks and awkward grins and half-whispered comments had irritated me. I was at loose ends. I wished someone would call, arrive, shout, send smoke signals. I wished something would *happen*. It felt like the air before a summer storm: oppressive, unnaturally still. It felt like the world was . . . pending.

When we reached Mather Street, I hesitated and then turned onto it toward Janet's apartment. Suddenly, I wanted very much to search it myself, to see what I could learn, which was probably nothing. Except possibly for one thing: money. According to the Plymouth Police, Terry and Janet had presumably robbed four stores in the Plymouth area that night. In three of them, they had tied up the owners and in the fourth had killed the old man. All told, it was estimated their night's take was around $1,400 to possibly $1,700 in cash. Where was it now?

Had it gone down in the bay with Terry? Maybe, but not likely. Assuming Janet shot Terry, she probably retrieved any proceeds he might have been holding from the night's work before dumping him overboard. Too bad for her she had missed his wallet in his inner jacket pocket. Although it had held very little money, it *had* held his ID. If he had remained unidentified, she might well have been home free. There was basically nothing that could easily have led to her.

Anyway, she wouldn't keep over a thousand dollars cash on her all the time, so it was probably somewhere in the apartment. If I found any money, that would give me some idea how much she did have with her and how far she could get before she either had to risk using a credit card or possibly try a robbery on her own.

I found myself at Mrs. Madeiros' back door and knocked, and knocked again until she finally heard me over the TV and opened the door. She'd known me since I was a pup, and I had little doubt she'd let me into Janet's place if I had some fairly reasonable explanation as to why I wanted in. I smiled sweetly and lied without a qualm: I had recently left a library book at Janet's that was due today. Janet had gone to Boston and wouldn't be back until late tonight. Could I please borrow the key?

Nobody in Ptown liked to return a library book late. It wasn't the twenty cents fine per day. Most of us could handle that. It was the sad, disappointed look of the librarian as she told you, "Others have been waiting for that book, dear. We really must be more thoughtful in the future, mustn't we?"

Mrs. Madeiros went for the bait and rummaged on a keyboard mounted near the door, finally handing me a key tied on a bright pink ribbon. "No need to bother me when you finish with it. Just leave it on the back porch, Alex. And be sure you get that book back today. They'll be trying to arrest her for that, next." She gave Fargo an absent pat and hurried back to Sally Jesse and her merry band of publicity-hungry psychopaths.

I put the key in the apartment lock and found it already unlocked. Janet was a trusting soul, apparently. The first things I saw were the flowers on the coffee table, but I managed to look quickly away.

Fargo was whuffling and exploring. I heard his nails click on the kitchen vinyl. That reminded me that there should be a couple of cold ones in the fridge. I popped one and then flopped into the easy chair, just to calm myself. I felt like a sneak thief. I unflopped rapidly from the lumpy, sprung springs in my butt. I moved to the dining table. The straight chairs at least looked safe. The peaches were still piled invitingly in the bowl. I didn't look at them, either. Beside them was a lined composition book, which I opened.

In Janet's neat, square handwriting was written:

> *Fargo*
> *Would like to put*
> *An embargo*
> *On sex*

I laughed, perhaps not a major poet, but a strong one. I flipped to the next page. It was entitled 'A Novel Novel' and under it was written:

*I'm supposed to be writing a novel, and for*
*a while I thought I mighty actually try it. How*
*silly, I've no idea even where to start. I guess*
*it should be autobiographical. Aren't most*
*first novels? Well, I can do that—and it*
*will be a very short book . . . 'She was born and*
*she tried very hard, but they would not let*
*her. The End.'*

Did she really feel that way? Was the whole world 'they'? What a heartbreakingly sad commentary on her life. How terrible to feel that the whole world was out to get you. She must have felt she was living beneath a giant fly swatter.

Beneath the 'Novel Novel' was a hurried scribble. "Alex, if you are reading this, know that I love you and pray for miracles." When the hell had she written that?

At that point the beers caught up with me and I walked into the bathroom. Rinsing my hands later, I realized there was no toothpaste or brush in evidence. And the little open glass shelves held no makeup, no mouthwash, hairbrush, comb, aspirin . . . no nothing. Damn! I stepped to the closet and slid open the door. Completely empty except for a ratty, saltwater stained, old sweatshirt on a hanger. I ran my hand along the top shelf back into the corner and nearly jumped out of my skin.

At first I thought I had picked up a small animal, but realized it was merely a soft, knitted watch cap.

I have a friend—a woman of a certain age—who swears that every woman immediately looks like a man when she dons a watch cap. I think that may be true of post-menopausal women who already look a bit androgynous. I'm not so sure of young, feminine women. Anyway, I would agree that as part of an overall disguise, to give a young woman a masculine air, it would be quite effective. I thought of my mental image of Janet yesterday and wondered what stories this cap could tell.

Turning to the bureau, I opened drawer after drawer. Empty, empty, empty. I slammed the last one shut and straightened up in utter confusion and frustration. When the hell had Janet emptied out her apartment? And where had she put everything?

Had she known she was going to take my car and run? Had she stashed her clothing somewhere to be picked up later? Had she destroyed it all as some possible evidence? Or did she actually have an accomplice who had taken the clothing and met her somewhere up Cape? Were they driving west together now, laughing at the simple Cape Cod rustics they had so thoroughly misled?

"Don't turn around, Alex, I have a gun. Don't make me use it. Put your hands on the bureau where I can see them."

I did as I was told, but risked a quick peek over my shoulder and found myself staring down the barrel of a Belgian Browning .32 automatic pointed directly at my spine.

# Chapter 14

Janet was no fool. She was about six feet away, giving me no chance to grab for the gun, even if I could work up the guts to try. I thought of trying to yank out a bureau drawer and throw it at her, but that would be clumsy. Probably I would just sprawl at her feet. The table lamp was out of reach. So a little light conversation seemed my only hope.

"Well! How did you get back here? I thought you'd be tooling down the road toward Seattle by now. Where's my car, by the way?" I told myself I was speaking casually, not exactly easy with a gun at your back.

"Safe and sound, parked right in there." She pointed at the wall in front of me.

"In the garage? Then where's Mrs. Madeiros' car?" Nothing made any sense.

"Around the corner. I knew yesterday you would head for a phone to have roadblocks put up at the bridges. I'm not angry, Alex.

It's simply what you would have to do. Believe me, I understand." She sounded almost serene, perhaps amused. And that scared me badly. "But I figured I'd have plenty of time to get back in this direction before you even made it to a phone, before anyone would look for me in any direction."

I heard the familiar smile in her voice and wondered if I were mad. "I knew Mrs. M. never locked up while she dozed through TV all afternoon," Janet explained. "So it was a cinch to lift the car keys off her board. She had mentioned she only used her car Sundays for church and Thursdays for errands. That gave me several days before she would realize it was gone or yours was here. So I just jockeyed the cars, threw a few things in hers and took off."

Despite my shaky position, I laughed. "I hope you didn't try to take off very fast."

She laughed back. "That car's not meant for the Daytona 500, is it?" Gee, we were getting more comfy by the minute. Could we split that other beer?

Plump Mrs. Madeiros, with her pouter-pigeon bosom, firmly curled white hair and thick glasses might look like everybody's grandmother, but secretly she was the poster girl for Demolition Derby. I guess the politically correct phrase would be mechanically challenged. Mrs. M. had never mastered the motor car. The Madeiros vehicle had left markings on about every roadside tree, bush, phone pole and street marker in town. And it had the scars to show for it. I had visions of a fleeing Janet, leaving a trail of metallic bread crumbs for us to follow—a side mirror falling off in Albany, a bumper guard in St. Louis, a door handle in Billings—as she putt-putted across America in search of Seattle and *Chez Veronique*.

"I don't understand, Janet. You could be cruising through Chicago as we speak. Why did you turn back?" One small part of me actually wished she'd made her escape a success. Most of me knew that she must be arrested and tried. All of me wished she were anywhere in the world except here . . . and now!

"The cops were at the bridge," Janet said. "They didn't give me a second look. Still, just their being there unnerved me. I got very shaky, I felt I was driving erratically. All I needed was to be conspicuous or have an accident. Across the bridge, I checked into one of those dinky motels." She stopped, as if she had answered my question.

"But you came back," I prompted. Even now, with all I knew and all I could reasonably surmise, I somehow hoped she might be miraculously innocent. I hoped she might say Terry had forced her cooperation at gun-point . . . and had videotape to prove it. I hoped she would say that in Stamford Sonny would find a real, live Janet look-alike—Jane Peaches—who had been Terry's actual conspirator. The pistol at my back? Even the most blameless sometimes resort to draconian measures to prove their innocence.

"Not right then. I ate something and tried to sleep, but I kept thinking . . . thinking. Thousands of thoughts jamming my mind. For example, I made myself a promise. When I open my restaurant, every morsel of good, tasty leftover food will go to a homeless shelter every day. Isn't that a good idea?"

"Excellent," I agreed. One of those little bribes we all offer God from time to time, but not terribly germane to this conversation, I added silently. I glanced back at Janet's face. Her expression was one of genuine altruism. How could she look so caring, so innocent? My mind felt blurry.

"Alex, I finally realized what had gone so wrong with my life. I've always put my faith in the wrong people, people who were *weak*. Remember? My school counselor. My mother. My commander, worrying about the brass. Terry, hoping *anybody* would take care of him. All weak. No strength among them. No wonder they all let me down."

She actually gave the gun a friendly little waggle. I cringed. "But you, Alex, were different. You didn't depend on anyone but yourself . . . and maybe a little bit on Fargo."

And I thought of Fargo. What would happen if she shot me? Of course Mom and Sonny would care for him, love him. But would he be happy? Wouldn't he miss me? I felt tears well up. Right then I would have gone on my knees and agreed to anything Janet wanted. Just let me live, live! But she was still touting her new-found philosophy of life.

"Yesterday, when you started talking about going to the police and lawyers, I really thought you had let me down like everyone else."

"Janet, I'll still try to help." I hoped my voice sounded reasonable and confident. "I mentioned this lawyer I know—"

"No, Alex. I know you'll help me when you understand. But not that kind of help. Once I explain how very little I was involved in this mess, you will understand and do what's right for us. You'll see. I was barely on the periphery. That's why I brought the gun in, so you would have to *listen* instead of talk. Please don't make me use it."

That was the second time she'd admonished me not to 'make' her use the gun. So, if she killed me, it would be *my* fault—the result of something I had done, or not done, to let her down. Well, nothing was ever Janet's fault. Why should that differ? And what was this "do what's best for *us*?" Did she really think we could continue? I didn't like the way this game was beginning to go. Janet was now using a new rule book, and only she had read it. I didn't know the rules but I knew I'd be dead if I strayed outside them.

"I was wondering, Janet. Did you and Terry stay together when you came back to Connecticut?" Nicely, Alex, nicely.

"We didn't know what to do except stay away from our families. We got a dreary apartment in Stamford and looked for jobs. Believe me, resigning 'for the good of the service' is not the best reference in the world. At last, Terry got a job he hated, teaching kids to sail at a yacht club in Darien. A daily reminder of what he had lost."

I tried to sound hearty. "I hope you had better luck." And screw Terry!

"Oh, sure! The only restaurants that would hire me were greasy spoons. I took a job as office manager at a used car place. Big title, little job. But the owners—Mr. and Mrs. Krause—were good to me. I reminded them of their daughter who had drowned a few years back. One nice perk, they let me take a car home off the lot every night."

This was sounding like her verbal tour of Seattle, but today I wasn't lying on a beach with a beer. My feet hurt. My neck and back were stiffening by the minute. My best plan now would be just to agree with everything she said, and hope to get her outdoors somehow so I could try to get that gun.

Her voice turned bitter. "The job didn't pay much. I'd never save enough for my restaurant. I saw myself in that dump forever, getting poorer and poorer. Terry was no help, he was sulky and drinking a lot . . . Oh!" She sounded distressed. I peeked around quickly, hoping she had dropped the gun or picked this fine moment for appendicitis.

"Oh, I just noticed. Your lovely flowers are wilting. One of us should have changed the water. Or put in an aspirin . . . my mama always said to put in an aspirin."

I actually lost my breath. Janet was disintegrating right before my eyes. Well, right behind my back. What mood would take her next? I did not want her upset. "It's spring. We'll have plenty more daffies." I forced a smile.

Janet looked at me blankly. "I was at my wit's end with Terry. Then one night I came home and found him sitting with sheets of paper and maps, cold sober and smiling. He said, 'Life screwed us, Janet, but we are about to screw life back. We shall have our bookstore and restaurant in Seattle.'"

Good ol' Terry! "I hope this plan was better than his last one."

Janet didn't hear my sarcasm. "Oh, it was! I would, as usual, take a car for the night or weekend. We would put stolen plates from all over on the car, drive to places he had picked out in New York, New Jersey—wherever. I would wear a man's disguise. Just before closing time, we would rob the small, isolated stores Terry had scouted out, change the license plates back to the legal ones and come home."

"And obviously it worked." Until one of you decided to kill an innocent old man.

"It was easy. I wasn't happy taking other people's money. But Terry assured me they were insured against this sort of thing, and wouldn't lose a penny. So you see," she finished brightly, "It was all Terry's idea, and no one would get hurt—even financially."

That wasn't what I had heard, and I wasn't sure these people would be insured against much of anything, but it didn't seem to be time to argue. I was still stalling. Where was the rest of the world? Couldn't Mrs. Madeiros stop by to borrow some sugar? Wasn't it time for the census takers? And where the hell were all those Jehovah's Witnesses when you needed them?

"I guess you knew about guns from the Coasties," I mentioned innocently. I was running out of creative conversation.

"Actually, I don't like guns. The first time Terry handed me this gun, I literally threw it back to him. I said I could never shoot anybody, never! 'You don't have to,' he assured me. 'You just have to look tough. Otherwise, nobody's going to hand us a till full of money.' He was right. We visited three stores, and it went off without a hitch. But, you see, even the gun was foisted onto me by Terry." She nodded emphatically, point scored.

I loved that—"visited three stores." It sounded like my mother doing her Christmas shopping. I tried once more to bring us back to some reality. "Janet, if we explain all this to . . . a friend," I said soothingly, "Surely all this background will help."

"You're beginning to irritate me, Alex. You have to understand! We weren't going to make this a lifetime career! We would just get the money we needed and put this time behind us. You know how little it meant to me? One weekend we were driving to do a little business, and I found myself enjoying the scenery and looking forward to dinner and a glass of wine. I wasn't really part of it at all! Terry planned everything, and, I regret to say, enjoyed every minute of it."

I shifted uncomfortably. "When did Terry start to foul things up?" Well, he had to "let her down" at some point, didn't he?

167

"Oh, he got into a mood. He wanted to stay in Connecticut and open a sports bar or an upscale gay club. I wanted out of Connecticut. I was afraid his bar buddies might get too interested in the source of his sudden investable money. Also, I had no thought of frying greasy hamburgers in the sweaty kitchen of some club while Terry sat out front and held court. I told him—if that was his plan, we would split the money—minus my original twenty-K—and go separate ways."

I smirked. "And how did that go down with Lord Fauntleroy?" I tried to flex my back unobtrusively. I had to make some move—and soon!

"He was livid, but then shrugged and laughed and said I was right. I should have known he was up to something. We agreed Plymouth would be our last little business. We put some clothes and all the money in an old duffel bag. I took an Acura that weekend. We planned to leave from Plymouth directly for Seattle, and we wanted a good car. I told the Krauses I needed a few days off due to a family illness. I was pretty sure by the time they realized I was gone for good, they'd feel so dim they wouldn't report it."

It was time to get rid of Terry. "Terry must have really screwed up in Plymouth."

"Everything that could go wrong did go wrong. We were leaving the liquor store. From out of nowhere, that stupid old man pulled a gun and fired at Terry. He missed but thought he hit him. He turned his gun on me. I had no choice but to shoot! Otherwise he would have shot me! I didn't want to kill the old coot! That was never in the plan. You can see that I had to do it, Alex, I had no choice. It was pure self-defense!"

For one split second I found myself believing her. The old man turned a gun on her. She fired in self-defense. Then of course I remembered that she and Terry already had two guns aimed at the old man and had also robbed him of his day's income Obviously, Janet's thinking had gone around some bend where I could not follow.

"We started to leave, and two young men—boys—were outside," she continued matter of factly. "We turned off some lights, hoping they would think he was closed. Terry wanted to kill them, but I pulled him away. I didn't want someone to hear gunfire or see them lying in the street. They hadn't paid attention to us, anyway. Still, I figured—being boys—they'd made the car, so I knew we couldn't use it for long."

"It's a good thing you were thinking straight," I prompted, "You went for a boat." I skipped over her casual comment about young bodies in the street.

"Yes. It was easy enough to get a boat, as you know. Terry wanted to take it into Boston, but I convinced him Boston would be the first place the police would look for us. I calculated we could come right across the bay—dock the boat at some wharf, where the residents had gone for the winter and just leave it to be found God-knows-when. We could lay low, while everybody looked for us in Boston."

I knew she was coming to the end of her tale and her options. How to stay one of her "good guys" was becoming hard. I felt like a fool. I felt used. I felt like I'd like to slap the hell out of her. And here I stood. What you might call a captive audience.

"About half way across the bay," Janet explained, "Terry went below to check around. He said we were taking on water. Later, he took the wheel and I went below to assess the water level and see if I could slow it down. The boat had been handling heavier and heavier. When I got below, I saw at once there was more water than the bilge pumps could handle, and I couldn't figure it out. Then it dawned on me that the bastard had opened the sea cocks. We were sinking. Then I understood. He was going to leave me to drown, while he took the money and got away in the Zodiac."

"But you caught him, apparently," I supplied.

"I ran topside and there he was. He had pulled the Zodiac alongside and was already in it—with the money. He had the Zodiac's motor idling and was bent over, starting to untie the line holding it to the Bertram."

169

"So you shot him."

"What else could I do? It was him or me. I couldn't just stand there and wait to drown! I had never expected him to let me down that way. It was an absolutely awful moment. When I fired, he pitched overboard and bumped along the side of the Bertram to the stern. Then there was this kind of *thunk!* And a little jolt when he hit the propeller." For the first time, her voice quavered. "I thought I was going to faint, but I managed to grab the line, jump into the Zodiac and pull away before the Bertram went under."

I risked another look and saw that she looked pained and unhappy, but there was nothing unsteady about the hand holding the gun. I caught a glance of Fargo, looking uneasy and confused. He was looking at the doorway, as if he'd seen someone or wanted to go out. So did I. "Then where did you come ashore?"

"Beach Point. I know this area, Alex. I beached the Zodiac, got the stuff out, secured the tiller and sent the boat back out to the middle of the bay. I hoped whoever found it would just keep it."

Her voice slowed now, in relief or fatigue. "I walked across the beach to the Holiday Inn. The night clerk was a half-asleep kid. I fed him some story about a fight with my boyfriend and running out in the storm, and got a room. I was about done in, not thinking well. I had to have rest. The next morning I went into town and got a few clothes and decided I'd better get out of a motel and find a small private place to stay, while I pulled myself together and planned what to do. The rest you know."

"Oh, yeah," I said bitterly, "I know the rest. The Peres family sure came in handy for keeping you updated, didn't we?"

"I know what you're thinking and I don't blame you." Her voice became gentle. "Yes, that's what it was at first. But then, something happened. I can hardly explain it. First, I began to like you—and Sonny, for that matter. Then I began to *really* like you. And everything seemed so *normal*. Going out to lunch, walking the dog, making dinner, and then Aunt Mae, asking me to tour the greenhouses. It was . . . it was like I was beginning to have, not only a lover, but the family I had always longed for." Her voice almost broke, and once again I almost believed her.

"I realized how truly unimportant all that other stuff had been. *This* was real. You, Fargo, your family. Us. I even thought of opening a restaurant here, so we could be together in the hometown you love so much. Then I realized that wouldn't be wise. It would be better to go to Seattle, as originally planned. So that's what we'll do. Now that you understand, we can make a life for *us*!"

It seemed to me we had a few details to clear up, but Janet had it all figured. "We'll take Mrs. M's car to your house tonight. I came by there earlier but you weren't home. I thought you might come here. It's why I left you the note in my notebook yesterday. We'll stay at your house tonight. You can get a rental car tomorrow— there's seventy-thousand dollars in that old grey mare parked out there, m'dear—but I really don't think we should try to take that particular horse across the country." Her voice was actually joyous. "Plenty to get us started out there. I'll buy my little restaurant and cook my heart out, and you'll start up your PI business and find all the sad, missing children."

"God, Janet. You've really got it all planned out, don't you?" I barely choked the words out, but apparently it was enough. Another peep over my shoulder showed a happy face, and I thought I saw the muzzle of the pistol drop an inch.

"I'm glad you do understand, darling. Believe me, we'll have a wonderful life out there. It's God's country . . . mountains, sea! Unfortunately," her voice dropped a tone, "I'm afraid Sonny can't be trusted to forget what he knows. So I guess before we go we'll have to . . . uh dispense with him and . . ."

"*What?*" I whirled around and things began to happen very fast. I felt a numbing blow to my side almost before I heard the crack of the pistol. Then I got a terrible pain in my head. Had she shot me twice? Why hadn't I heard two reports?

Then I really didn't much care one way or the other. I was too busy diving into a very deep, very black hole.

171

# Chapter 15

God was speaking to me in a deep, far-away voice. "Wake up, Alexandra, come on now, it's time to wake up."

"Thank you, Sir, but I'd rather sleep," I croaked. I tried to look at Him, but couldn't seem to get my eyes open.

He began to shake my arm gently. "No more sleeping, my dear. It's time to wake up, now."

My dear, that sounded nice. It boded well for the future. I managed to open one eye, the other seemed glued shut. I saw that He was wearing a grey pin-stripe suit and polished black wingtips—sartorially correct, I noted, and none of this old-fashioned flowing white robe and scruffy sandals stuff. And I saw that the hand that shook me was old and gnarled—well, that was appropriate, wasn't it? Suddenly Fargo was beside me, licking at my face. Fargo, had she shot him, too? She must have. He was here. My dog was here . . . with me! How wonderful!

God bellowed, "Get that beast away from that wound!" I heard a clatter of feet and saw two shiny black boots topped by a pair of wrinkled khakis. Sonny! How did Sonny get here with Fargo and me in Heaven? At least, I guessed we were in Heaven.

"Heaven?" I asked, as Sonny pulled on my arms.

"No, you're not heavy," he snapped, "But you're not helping, either. Now come on. Help me get you up." He got his hands under my arms and lifted me to my feet and sort of danced me over to one of the chairs at the table. I looked around me and saw my brother and Dr. Marsten looking at me with concern.

"All awake now?" The doctor asked, I nodded and thought my head fell off. "Good. Let me just get a fresh paper towel and dampen it, so I can clean you up and see what we've got here."

Now fully aware I wasn't in Heaven, I realized I was in Janet's apartment and very much alive. Of course, I was under Doc Marsten's care, so that fact could change momentarily. I snarled softly at Sonny. "What the hell is *he* doing here?"

"Can't help it. Both EMT crews are tied up over on Route Six at a head-on collision," he whispered. "Just be nice."

"Why? Ouch!" Marsten cleaned the blood away from my eye and forehead and revealed a fairly deep cut just over my eyebrow. "Don't you dare stitch that without an anesthetic!" I shrilled. "I want some of that stuff that freezes it, do you hear?"

Everybody heard. The room went quiet, and I realized that in addition to Sonny and Marsten, there were two cops milling around the living area and another cop—this one female—sitting with Janet in two chairs that had been moved into the tiny kitchen. Janet cradled her right wrist in her left hand, and I could see she was in pain.

But it was the hurt-angry-sulky expression on her face that thoroughly jolted me. I had seen it again and again as she talked of her parents, her counselor, her commander, Terry. And now I had joined the legions of those who had "let her down." She had to know the Seattle restaurant dream was well and truly dead. And it could not be her fault. It could *never* be her fault. That would negate its very existence. It had to be my fault. I suppose the only way I could have atoned would have been to die from her gunshot. I felt very tired.

I turned back to Marsten. "Oh," I muttered, embarrassed. "Well, might as well make it painless if possible, huh?"

"I wouldn't have it any other way, my dear. This is not the Dark Ages. We are considerably more enlightened these days." He smiled knowingly and reached into his bag, coming up with a little aerosol can. Guarding my eye with one hand he sprayed the cut with something that made it feel cold, then numb. He leaned over me with needle and thread, and I thought I saw a slight tremor in his hand. Oh, God, I thought, he's liable to sew my nose to my ear. He must have read my mind.

"Not to worry, now, Alex. I sew a very fine seam, as the ladies used to say." And so he did. I was together, neat and bandaged in short order. "There, now, all done. Just stop by in about a week and I'll take out the stitches for you. Three months and there won't even be a hairline scar to remind you that it happened. Now, let's just be sure you're not concussed."

He did the bit of asking how many fingers I saw, and he shined a flashlight in my eyes, which hurt, and told me if I vomited or got double vision to call him at once. Yeah. Well, maybe, in a pig's eye. "Now," he asked. "Anything else need my attention?"

"No, thank you, Doctor . . . oh, yes, my God, I forgot. My side! That's where she shot me first, in my side."

Doc Marsten looked startled and confused. "There's no blood there . . . you say you're shot . . . exactly where . . . how can . . . ?"

Sonny chimed in. "Janet only fired one shot and that went wide. She didn't actually shoot you at all, Alex. Just as she fired, Fargo leaped from out of nowhere and hit you in the side and knocked you out of the line of fire. Fargo hit you. He saved your life!"

Sonny turned to Marsten. "Doc, you never saw anything like it! That dog is so smart, he knew he had to get Alex away from where that bullet would go, and as Janet fired he hit Alex and knocked her aside into the table, but that's better than a bullet! He's some brave, clever dog!"

I wondered how Sonny knew all this, but somehow I just couldn't quite pull it together to ask him. Explanations could wait. I was alive. So was Sonny. So was Fargo. It was enough for now.

"A noble beast," Marsten agreed unenthusiastically. "But let's look at the side anyway." He pulled up my shirt and expertly felt my left rib cage. "There's no wound and I don't feel anything. Breathe deep. Does that hurt? No? Cough. Does that hurt? No, well, no broken ribs. Maybe a bruise, but nothing serious."

I was beginning to like his type of medicine. It was certainly simpler, faster and God knows cheaper than the X-rays, MRI's and CAT scans I'd have gotten at the hospital. Perhaps I had misjudged him. He turned to Sonny.

"Still, she's had quite a shock. If there is any wine or brandy around, a small glass wouldn't hurt."

How had I ever not realized what a fine old physician he really was? "There's wine on the kitchen counter," I advised them.

"I'll get it," Sonny said. "Doc, you'd better come and have a look at our shooter in here. I think maybe I broke her wrist."

I sipped the wine Sonny had fetched, and watched them go to Janet. Dr. Marsten bent over her arm. He seemed to be speaking gently to her, and for some reason that made me want to cry. Sonny came back out and fired off a bunch of orders to his minions.

"Santos, you and Highsmith get Mrs. Madeiros' car towed to the impound lot. Get that money out of the trunk and take it into the jail and lock it in a cell. I want somebody sitting outside that cell watching it till I get there and we can count it and get it to the state police. Fingerprint the duffel bag inside and out and see if you can get any prints off the bills. With luck you'll get Janet's and O'Malley's and some of the store owners they robbed. I especially hope for the old man in Plymouth. Get Alex's car taken in, too. She can come by tomorrow and give us her fingerprints to disqualify."

"My prints are on file in Boston," I said. "For my license."

"Okay, then we'll get them off the computer in the morning. Mitch, wait here for me, please, I'll need you in a minute." Mitch sat gingerly in the easy chair, and Sonny went, at my request, for another glass of wine.

I looked idly around the room and spotted the bowl of peaches. Suddenly, it seemed terribly important to me that someone enjoy them. I didn't want them anymore, couldn't bear the thought of them, but someone must have them. "Jeanine," I called to the female cop.

"Yes, Alex." She came over and stooped beside me. "You okay, honey? Can I do anything for you?"

Ordinarily I don't like the casual 'honey,' but Jeanine was a warm-hearted young woman who would be another Mrs. Madeiros in thirty years, so I didn't make any smart retort. "Jeanine, I bought those peaches yesterday afternoon, and I really don't think I can eat a thing. But they are too beautiful to waste. I want you to take them home for you and the kids."

"Well . . ."

"Please, you'll be doing me a favor." You see, I could have added, the daffodils are wilting, and Janet is going away. Let's at least save those gorgeous peaches. It made perfect sense to me.

"Well, if you insist. They sure are beauties and we'll all love them." She looked into the kitchen and then at me. "I can understand they might not set well with you, honey." She took the bowl into the kitchen.

Dr. Marsten came out and confirmed that Janet had a broken wrist, that he had put it in a soft cast and given her some painkillers and provided Jeanine additional ones to give her later. He patted both Fargo and me on the head with similar disinterested kindness, bowed a courtly goodnight and left, followed by Janet and Jeanine, who said goodnight and thanked me for the peaches as if we had all been at a neighborhood quilting bee. Janet stared straight ahead, pale, composed, pouting and seemingly unaware of anyone in the room.

I started to stand up and go to her, but cancelled the move. There was no "her" and "me" anymore.

Sonny turned to Mitch. "Go with them. Get Janet booked and settled, and make her as comfortable as you can. On your way out, drape some crime scene tape around here. Otherwise Mrs. M's snoopy son-in-law will be in here collecting souvenirs—and probably selling them. Tell Mrs. M. everyone is okay and her property isn't damaged. Give her the key but tell her she can't come in or disturb anything for a while. I should be back at the station in—oh, no more than an hour."

Mitch nodded, told me he was glad I was okay and walked out stiffly—no doubt from his sojourn in the easy chair.

Sonny came back out and sat down, filching one of my cigarettes and blowing a cloud of smoke wearily toward the ceiling. I raised my eyebrows but said nothing. There was a question I had to ask, and it mortified me. "You've known this for a while, haven't you?" I finally got it out.

"Well, maybe part of it. You see," he said, "I found out a couple of days ago that Janet probably stayed at the Holiday Inn."

"I thought you had all the motels checked out earlier."

"I did. Sanchez went around. But he asked the clerks if any unusual-acting *men* had checked in that night or the next morning. Nothing specifically about women. The dopey kid who was night clerk at the Holiday Inn said the only two men who registered that night were regulars—salesmen who come every month. He didn't bother to mention that a half-drowned woman dragging a fifty-pound duffel bag had crawled in and paid cash about three a.m. of the morning in question. When I found out Sanchez hadn't asked about women, he went back again and the clerk told him about Janet."

"How did you know to come here?" I asked.

"Oh, that was easy enough," he smiled. "It was my timing that was poor. Well, let's see where we are. Yesterday morning, the Stonington Police sent through a fax on Terrence's background, which included serving in the Coast Guard. That was just one coincidence too many around Janet."

I nodded. "Yes, Janet told me about that—was it yesterday? I'm all screwed up. God, Sonny, what an idiot you picked for a sister. She had me completely fooled."

He smiled, but nicely. "Well, she had a lot of us fooled. You, me. Aunt Mae told Mother she was 'a delight.' I suppose you know Mrs. M. wouldn't let Jeanine and Mitch in here. Said she refused to believe Janet was a criminal and that she felt sorry for Mitch if he had nothing better to do than look at Janet's intimate clothing. Don't feel too bad."

"Yeah. I guess so. Anyway, you went to Stonington."

"On a hunch, to see if maybe talking to his mother in person would help. I thought she might be calmer now and remember something important. I didn't get much. She really is an airhead. She stuck to Jane Peaches being the name of his girlfriend, even when I mentioned Janet Meacham, but she did settle on Stamford as being where he lived. Which was no help, Stamford is a sizeable city."

It occurred to me that Sonny and I had found out much of the same information at about the same time. Of course I had garnered my facts either lying on a beach drinking beer or standing with a gun at my back. Still, I wondered what sort of fool he must think me. There had been a collage of early warning signals I had ignored. Thank God he had not.

"While I was there," he said. "I talked to some of the state police guys at the troop barracks. They took me out for a late lunch, being nice to the poor rube cop. But they didn't know even as much as I did about what had recently turned up. I went back to the barracks to get my car, and lo and behold, a make had come in on the Acura used in Plymouth. A guy named Allingham had sold it to a Stamford used car dealer Stamford. It seemed legitimate, but confusing. I mean, obviously the car wasn't still sitting in the dealer's lot, it's impounded in Plymouth. So why hadn't the dealer either filed papers that he had sold it and to whom, or reported it stolen?"

"Unless he was in on the robberies, too, would have been my first thought," I said, amazed at how collected I sounded. "But that's wrong. I don't think he was." Something nagged at me, a memory just out of reach about cars.

Sonny nodded. "We all figured the dealer was part of it, too. The state cops saw no need to go all the way down there that night. They said they'd look into it Monday." Sonny shook his head sadly at this example of out-of-state cooperation. "That ticked me off a little. I thought it was more urgent than that. I was beginning to get very uneasy about Ms. Peaches. I figured most car lots stay open pretty late, and I could make it down there if I pushed it." He ground his cigarette out.

"I did, but they were closed. I didn't know car dealers close Sundays in Connecticut. Wouldn't you think someone might have mentioned it?" When Sonny starts bitching about other cops, you know he's tired.

"Well, I decided since I was down there, I'd see if I could locate Mr. Allingham and hear what he had to say about the Acura. I found the offbeat little suburb where he lived, and found Allingham, finally, in the Episcopal Church there."

"Looking for sanctuary?" I asked.

"Him or me? No, he's the rector of the church. Nice man. He had me to his house next door for a drink. Believe me, by then I needed one. He told me about the people who owned the car lot, name of Krause. They'd been his neighbors for years, salt of the earth. He said the only thing about them that might be dishonest was they probably gave him too much money for the Acura. Apparently Allingham's wife died some months back, and a few weeks ago he sold her car, since he no longer needed two."

My head hurt. I felt as if I could go to sleep right there in an upright chair. Sonny looked at me sharply. "How you doing?"

"Tired," I said. "And feeling like the dolt of the century. The more I hear, the dumber I feel. My luck with women goes from the bad to the ridiculous."

"That's exactly right—luck. It had nothing to do with you. And luck always changes in the long run."

"Sometimes you really can be sensitive, Sergeant." I was feeling weepy and didn't want it to show.

"Yeah, well." He cleared his throat. "Now about the Krauses. Allingham told me they lost a daughter to drowning not long ago. He said how happy they'd been to meet a young woman who was a lot like their kid, even looked like her. It thrilled them that she took a job they had open. Guess who?"

Suddenly I remembered what Janet had told me on the beach. Where was my brain? "Janet! I forgot—she told me yesterday about borrowing cars from a job she had."

"Yep. They let her use a car off the lot, just being nice. Last week she said she had to drive to New Hampshire regarding some family illness and asked for a car in good shape for the trip. They gave her the Acura. Worry really set in when she wasn't back by mid-week. With no idea where to reach her, they mentioned it to the minister. They didn't want to call the police and embarrass her if nothing was wrong."

"Is there anybody nice she *didn't* take advantage of?" I sounded peevish.

"Not that I know." Sonny grinned. "I wanted to go see the Krauses right then. Allingham said it was late, asked me not to go till morning. I guess the wife hasn't been strong since her daughter's death."

"Did Allingham put you up?"

"No, I went back to Stamford and checked into a hotel, for which—given the price—I am very glad I can bill the town of Provincetown!"

"I'll never tell you ordered breakfast in bed."

He looked both startled and guilty. Do I know my brother or what? I wanted to laugh at his discomfort, but I didn't dare. I had a feeling I might not stop.

"So," he continued, "I met with the Krauses this morning. They were chagrined, but essentially told the same story Allingham had.

Even now they insisted it was nothing more than a delay with some reasonable explanation."

I felt tears well up and wondered whom they were for. The Krauses? Janet? Me?

I blinked them back, hoping Sonny wouldn't notice.

"And can you believe it," he mused, "when I told them she would now be wanted for questioning in a robbery and double murder. They insisted I was dead wrong. And then added they would hire her the best defense lawyer they could find!"

"Well," I said wistfully, "She was nice in a way."

"Yes." Sonny's voice was gentle. "She was." It then occurred to me we were both using the past tense.

"How much of this little drama did you witness?" I cleared my throat and waved my hand around the room.

"Most of it. I hot-footed it back here. When I found out Janet hadn't been apprehended and that Mrs. M. had balked at a search, I got worried. I just had a feeling she was in town somewhere. But first, I thought I'd just cruise by here and see if the lights were on or if—God forbid—she was at your place. Then I noticed the Madeiros car parked around the corner."

I was fading fast. Maybe a cigarette would help. I pulled the pack and lighter back from Sonny's side of the table. I wondered idly what number of today's allotted five this one was? I stifled a giggle. What was wrong with me?

"I knew the Lady M. wouldn't park on the street when she had a perfectly good garage waiting for her, if she could just get inside it without taking off a fender. So I called in and told Mitch to get some people to sit on her car and to seal off the block just in case we had trouble. I walked up the drive, and could see the whole thing through the window. What would have happened if Mrs. Madeiros had wandered over to bring her a pie, I cringe to think." He stretched his hands in front of him and cracked his knuckles, which irritated the hell out of me.

"Once inside the little entry, I was afraid Fargo would jump up and give the whole thing away. Thank God, he was only interested in you. He looked at me once, but you were what he was focused on. He just kept staring at you, looking worried, obviously planning his move. Man, that dog!" I couldn't help the laugh that escaped me. My brave, beloved Fargo!

Sonny gave me an odd look before continuing. "I'm not sure you really appreciate that dog."

I knew I could never tell him quite how much. I just fondled Fargo's ear and nodded to Sonny to continue.

"Anyway, I couldn't move closer to get a good firing angle. I didn't dare startle her in any way. You can't tell what an amateur will do with a gun. I was afraid to shoot her from where I was for fear the bullet would go right through her and into you. I was well and truly stuck. Then Fargo leaped and knocked you aside a nano-second before she fired. He must have sensed she was going to. I jumped her and got her gun. That's that."

That wasn't quite that. I knew perfectly well what Fargo had done. Perhaps he *had* sensed she was going to shoot. But he hadn't soared across the room to push me out of the way. He had felt the building tension and was scared to death, and tried to jump into my arms.

My creampuff.

Of course he had saved my life willy-nilly, and he was the love of my life always. He would go down in the annals of Provincetown as the world's bravest dog.

And no one would ever know different except the creampuff and me—and we wouldn't care. We were together. I leaned down and hugged him and tried to smother my tears. But not before Sonny saw them. Damn. And then he reached across and tousled my hair and handed me his handkerchief. Oh, hell, now I was really crying.

Sonny reached out an awkward hand to help me up and held my coat for me, probably for the first time in our lives. "I'll take you home in my car and see you tucked in," he said. "Your car will have to be checked for prints and all that stuff. Give me the keys and I'll get it to you at some point."

"Fine," I agreed. "Oh, I guess the keys are in it, or Janet has them. I don't." We started down the driveway, Sonny holding Fargo's leash. The chilly air was fresh and just slightly damp against my aching head. It felt good. "Sonny, I know you've got a long night in front of you, but would you mind if we walked home? I feel fuzzy. Maybe the air would do me good. And I'm sure poor Fargo badly needs some outdoor time."

"Sure. No problem. Unless you'd like to spend the night at Mom's? I can get my car later. Let's hope nobody steals it. I think I left the keys in it. Larry Cole would have a stroke."

"He's already had one, thanks to me, bless his miserly little heart. And, no thanks, I'd rather just go home. I'll call Mom and let her know I'm okay."

I saw Mrs. Madeiros standing on her back porch, alert and watchful, and imagined she would find her soap operas somewhat tame after this evening's action. She looked as if she had been crying.

# Chapter 16

It had grown dark as we turned up Commercial Street. Under a streetlight, I had checked my watch and was surprised to see it was after eight o'clock. I think I was still somewhere back in the late afternoon.

The streets were quiet on an off-season Monday night, few cars, fewer still pedestrians. That didn't displease me. I wasn't ready to face the world or be around much noise quite yet. I was still trying to digest everything that had happened, and obviously it was not going to be a speedy process.

I could see that Fargo's leash was taut. Doubtless he knew exactly what time it was and would like to get home to his dinner. Come to think of it, I felt empty myself, but I wasn't sure it was hunger.

Probably not surprisingly, my legs were wobbly and I felt slightly light-headed—if you can feel light-headed with a clanging headache. I couldn't seem to get a handle on my thoughts. My head spun, and I did think Doc Marsten had missed a concussion.

A few feet ahead was one of the park benches the town has thoughtfully placed along the sidewalk for footsore tourists. I aimed for it, saying I'd like to rest a minute and have a cigarette. Sonny was surprisingly agreeable for a man with a long drive behind him and a busy night ahead. In fact, he'd actually been nice for something over three hours now, which must be some kind of record for us. Fargo sat on the bench between us, making sure he was touching us both. He'd had a rough day, too.

As I lit a cigarette, Sonny pulled a bottle of wine from his duffel pocket. "I figured this was yours and there was no reason to leave it there," he explained. Actually I had given it to Janet a few days back, in case she needed creative inspiration at some point. But I doubted its ownership would come under question now.

From another pocket he took one of those knives that has every-thing on it but a blade. He finally found the corkscrew and opened the bottle. Now that was really thoughtful of him, I smiled to myself. But he took a long pull on the bottle and rested it on his knee with no sign of offering me a sip. Well, nobody's perfect.

"Nice wine," he commented. "What is it?"

I took the bottle and a good swallow before I answered. "Of course it's nice. It's a good claret . . . a companionable little wine with just a hint of sassiness to . . ."

"Oh, shut up, Alex. Unless you read the label or the wine list you wouldn't know Burgundy from Tokay!"

"Sure I would. Burgundy is a real dark red and Tokay . . ."

"You know what I meant. Anyway, are you okay?"

I'd have to be a whole lot worse before I'd admit it to my brother. "Oh, I think so. My head aches and I'm shaky. But I'll live. And that reminds me, it sounds kind of pompous, but thank you for saving my life."

"I told you, it's Fargo who saved your life. I have never seen anything like that. I don't think I'll ever get over it." Hearing his name, Fargo turned toward Sonny and whuffled on his cheek.

"Maybe the first round goes to Fargo," I conceded, "But I rather imagine Janet would have fired again, and I doubt she would have missed her target a second time at that distance. So I am twice saved, once by Fargo and once by you." Now the dog turned back toward me and panted on *my* cheek. "Dammit, Fargo, this is not a bloody tennis match."

Sonny laughed and scratched the dog's neck. "Whatever. But what I meant before was, are you going to be okay . . . uh, about Janet?"

I was surprised at how calm and objective I managed to sound. "Not hardly. Only yesterday I was the love of her life. Today she casually takes a shot at me—after begging me to run away with her into the sunset and, oh, yes, by-the-by, to dispense with my brother. My God, Sonny, is my head injury a little more serious than Doctor Marsten diagnosed, or is there something just a tiny bit wrong with this picture?"

"Oh, I think your head is okay—as much as it ever is." He could only be so nice for so long. "Of course something is wrong with the picture. To me she sounded so deep into denial she was almost coming up in China. I'm sure there's some ten-syllable psychological word for it. I think the bottom line is that Janet looked on that damn restaurant of hers as an escape from everything she hated and a symbol of everything she had ever wanted to be. Nothing was ever her fault, did you notice?"

"Well, she did have a rough time as a kid." I disagreed weakly.

"Bullshit. I get pretty sick of that argument. So they were poor. We were not exactly the rich and famous, and I can remember some parts of childhood that weren't a *Leave It To Beaver* rerun. Thousands of kids don't have a storybook life, but they don't grow up to be murderers, either."

"I suppose. But I just can't reconcile it. She could be gentle, interesting, tender, smart—that's what I saw, anyway." She was also funny, sweet, passionate, I added to myself.

"Yesterday we had a picnic on the beach before she took the car." Even now I could not say *stole* the car. "She told me that she loved me. I believed her. I do believe her. Maybe I didn't quite love her—yet—or maybe I did, but I certainly *cared* a lot."

I looked at Sonny, still unable to believe what I was saying. "A week ago, she committed a robbery and didn't hesitate to kill when her partner was threatened by the old man, and kill again when she was threatened by the partner!"

I lit cigarette number two hundred and ten. "You may have heard her, Sonny. She denied any complicity in anything. It was all Terry—backed up by everyone from a school counselor to the Seattle cops. Not one bit of it was her. I think *she* thinks she really just went along for the ride. That's crazy, Sonny."

"Maybe. She's no fool and it could be a very good defense strategy, or just self-centered and manipulative. She didn't care who she used—or how—to get what she wanted. She starts a career of robbing people to get money for the restaurant. When Terry becomes a problem, she's ready to get rid of him in a heartbeat."

Sonny took another swig from the bottle. Probably not recommended for public servants sitting on a public bench. "Finally, Alex, she meets you. Everything is great. You're great. Your family is great. Until her past starts to catch up. Once threatened, she'd kill us all. Hell, she would have poisoned the town water supply if she thought it would get her that fucking chophouse!"

I sighed. "You're right, of course. Everything you say makes sense. It's just that when I think of her, I kind of think of two people. I can't believe she was both of them."

"You know what she reminds me of, Alex? A woman who really, really wants a baby. She gets pregnant." He grinned. "At least we can hope that part is pleasant. But then she has morning sickness, feels lousy, gets backaches, can't sleep. She spends hours in labor. But every woman I've ever heard talk about it says when she sees that baby, she forgets all about pain. She's got her baby—it was worth it."

"Gee, Dad, I didn't know you cared."

"I'm right! Janet was like that with the damned restaurant. If you and she had miraculously got to Seattle, she would have put this all away and assumed you would, too. She'd have got her restaurant, been a law-abiding citizen, lived happily ever after."

"Maybe. Unless some night she machined gunned me and a crowd of customers because we forgot to compliment the soup."

Knowing I didn't want to say it, knowing I would never say it, I blurted, "Good God, Sonny I've been sleeping with a *murderer*!" And I burst into tears.

"No. You have not. You were sleeping with a bright, pretty, appealing young woman. You encountered the murderer later." He took my chin in his hand and made me look at him. "It is extremely important, Alex, that you remember that." He sounded very serious. I wanted to believe him. One day I would.

"Yeah, I guess." I sniffed back the tears. "What was it Bogart said in *Casablanca*? 'Of all the gin joints in all the world, she had to walk into mine.'"

"Something like that." He took another pull on the wine and remembered to hand it to me.

I took a sip and kept the bottle. Sgt. Peres had had enough. He would not be early to bed this night.

He stirred slightly. "Of course I know what Harmon would say."

"*Harmon*? What the hell could he have to say about this mess?"

Sonny gave a credible imitation of Harmon's high-pitched, raspy voice. "Them two Peres kids never did have no luck with women. Hell, even th' dog's fixed, so he can't have no luck neither."

Sonny giggled. I snickered. We both burst into laughter. Fargo joined his wonderful vibrant bass to our baritone and alto. And the three of us sat on a park bench and sent little white balloons rising into the cold quiet air of an early spring night.

# ABOUT THE AUTHOR

Jessica Thomas is a native of Chattanooga, Tennessee, where she attended Girls' Preparatory School. She later graduated cum laude from Bard College, Annandale-on-Hudson, New York, with a bachelor's degree in literature.

After an early retirement, Miss Thomas spent a bit of time doing some rather dull freelance assignments and ghostwriting two totally depressing self-help books, always swearing someday that she would write something that was just plain fun. When her friend, Marian Pressler "gave" her Alex and Fargo, Jessica took them immediately to heart and ran right to her keyboard.

Miss Thomas makes her home in Connecticut with her almost-cocker spaniel, Woofer. Her hobbies include gardening, reading, and animal protection activities.

Publications from
# BELLA BOOKS, INC.
*The best in contemporary lesbian fiction*

P.O. Box 10543, Tallahassee, FL 32302
Phone: 800-729-4992
www.bellabooks.com

CAUGHT IN THE NET by Jessica Thomas. 188 pp. A wickedly observant story of mystery, danger, and love in Provincetown.                ISBN 1-931513-54-6    $12.95

DREAMS FOUND by Lyn Denison. 201 pp. Australian Riley embarks on a journey to meet her birth mother . . . and gains not just a family but the love of her life. ISBN 1-931513-58-9    $12.95

A MOMENT'S INDISCRETION by Peggy J. Herring. Jackie is torn between her better judgment and the overwhelming attraction she feels for Valerie.      ISBN 1-931513-59-7    $12.95

DEATH BY DEATH by Claire McNab. 216 pp. 5th Denise Cleever Thriller.                ISBN 1-931513-34-1    $12.95

IN EVERY PORT by Karin Kallmaker. 224 pp. Jessica's sexy, adventuresome travels.            ISBN 1-931513-36-8    $12.95

TOUCHWOOD by Karin Kallmaker. 240 pp. Loving May/December romance.          ISBN 1-931513-37-6    $12.95

WATERMARK by Karin Kallmaker. 248 pp. One burning question . . . how to lead her back to love?
                ISBN 1-931513-38-4    $12.95

EMBRACE IN MOTION by Karin Kallmaker. 240 pp. A whirlwind love affair.          ISBN 1-931513-39-2    $12.95

ONE DEGREE OF SEPARATION by Karin Kallmaker.
232 pp. Can an Iowa City librarian find love and passion
when a California girl surfs into the close-knit dyke
capital of the Midwest?                  ISBN 1-931513-30-9    $12.95

CRY HAVOC A Detective Franco Mystery by Baxter Clare.
240 pp. A dead hustler with a headless rooster in his lap sends Lt.
L.A. Franco headfirst against Mother Love.
                                  ISBN 1-931513931-7    $12.95

DISTANT THUNDER by Peggy J. Herring. 294 pp.
Bankrobbing drifter Cordy awakens strange new feelings in Leo in
this romantic tale set in the Old West.
                                  ISBN 1-931513-28-7    $12.95

COP OUT by Claire McNab. 216 pp. 4th Detective Inspector
Carol Ashton Mystery.             ISBN 1-931513-29-5    $12.95

BLOOD LINK by Claire McNab. 159 pp. 15th Detective
Inspector Carol Ashton Mystery. Is Carol unwittingly playing
into a deadly plan?               ISBN 1-931513-27-9    $12.95

TALK OF THE TOWN by Saxon Bennett. 239 pp.
With enough beer, barbecue and B.S., anything
is possible!                      ISBN 1-931513-18-X    $12.95

MAYBE NEXT TIME by Karin Kallmaker. 256 pp. Sabrina
Starling has it all: fame, money, women—and pain. Nothing hurts
like the one that got away.       ISBN 1-931513-26-0    $12.95

WHEN GOOD GIRLS GO BAD: A Motor City Thriller by
Therese Szymanski. 230 pp. Brett, Randi, and Allie join forces
to stop a serial killer.          ISBN 1-931513-11-2    $12.95

A DAY TOO LONG: A Helen Black Mystery by Pat Welch.
328 pp. This time Helen's fate is in her own hands.
                                  ISBN 1-931513-22-8    $12.95

THE RED LINE OF YARMALD by Diana Rivers. 256 pp.
The Hadra's only hope lies in a magical red line . . . climactic
sequel to *Clouds of War*.        ISBN 1-931513-23-6    $12.95

OUTSIDE THE FLOCK by Jackie Calhoun. 224 pp. Jo embraces her new love and life. ISBN 1-931513-13-9 $12.95

LEGACY OF LOVE by Marianne K. Martin. 224 pp. Read the whole Sage Bristo story. ISBN 1-931513-15-5 $12.95

STREET RULES: A Detective Franco Mystery by Baxter Clare. 304 pp. Gritty, fast-paced mystery with compelling Detective L.A. Franco ISBN 1-931513-14-7 $12.95

RECOGNITION FACTOR: 4th Denise Cleever Thriller by Claire McNab. 176 pp. Denise Cleever tracks a notorious terrorist to America. ISBN 1-931513-24-4 $12.95

NORA AND LIZ by Nancy Garden. 296 pp. Lesbian romance by the author of *Annie on My Mind*. ISBN 1931513-20-1 $12.95

MIDAS TOUCH by Frankie J. Jones. 208 pp. Sandra had everything but love. ISBN 1-931513-21-X $12.95

BEYOND ALL REASON by Peggy J. Herring. 240 pp. A romance hotter than Texas. ISBN 1-9513-25-2 $12.95

ACCIDENTAL MURDER: 14th Detective Inspector Carol Ashton Mystery by Claire McNab. 208 pp. Carol Ashton tracks an elusive killer. ISBN 1-931513-16-3 $12.95

SEEDS OF FIRE: Tunnel of Light Trilogy, Book 2 by Karin Kallmaker writing as Laura Adams. 274 pp. Intriguing sequel to *Sleight of Hand*. ISBN 1-931513-19-8 $12.95

DRIFTING AT THE BOTTOM OF THE WORLD by Auden Bailey. 288 pp. Beautifully written first novel set in Antarctica. ISBN 1-931513-17-1 $12.95

CLOUDS OF WAR by Diana Rivers. 288 pp. Women unite to defend Zelindar! ISBN 1-931513-12-0 $12.95

DEATHS OF JOCASTA: 2nd Micky Knight Mystery by J.M. Redmann. 408 pp. Sexy and intriguing Lambda Literary Award-nominated mystery. ISBN 1-931513-10-4 $12.95

LOVE IN THE BALANCE by Marianne K. Martin. 256 pp. The classic lesbian love story, back in print!
ISBN 1-931513-08-2    $12.95

THE COMFORT OF STRANGERS by Peggy J. Herring. 272 pp. Lela's work was her passion . . . until now.
ISBN 1-931513-09-0    $12.95

CHICKEN by Paula Martinac. 208 pp. Lynn finds that the only thing harder than being in a lesbian relationship is ending one.
ISBN 1-931513-07-4    $11.95

TAMARACK CREEK by Jackie Calhoun. 208 pp. An intriguing story of love and danger.
ISBN 1-931513-06-6    $11.95

DEATH BY THE RIVERSIDE: 1st Micky Knight Mystery by J.M. Redmann. 320 pp. Finally back in print, the book that launched the Lambda Literary Award-winning Micky Knight mystery series.
ISBN 1-931513-05-8    $11.95

EIGHTH DAY: A Cassidy James Mystery by Kate Calloway. 272 pp. In the eighth installment of the Cassidy James mystery series, Cassidy goes undercover at a camp for troubled teens.
ISBN 1-931513-04-X    $11.95

MIRRORS by Marianne K. Martin. 208 pp. Jean Carson and Shayna Bradley fight for a future together.
ISBN 1-931513-02-3    $11.95

THE ULTIMATE EXIT STRATEGY: A Virginia Kelly Mystery by Nikki Baker. 240 pp. The long-awaited return of the wickedly observant Virginia Kelly.
ISBN 1-931513-03-1    $11.95

FOREVER AND THE NIGHT by Laura DeHart Young. 224 pp. Desire and passion ignite the frozen Arctic in this exciting sequel to the classic romantic adventure *Love on the Line*.
ISBN 0-931513-00-7    $11.95

WINGED ISIS by Jean Stewart. 240 pp. The long-awaited sequel to *Warriors of Isis* and the fourth in the exciting Isis series.
ISBN 1-931513-01-5    $11.95

ROOM FOR LOVE by Frankie J. Jones. 192 pp. Jo and Beth must overcome the past in order to have a future together.
ISBN 0-9677753-9-6     $11.95

THE QUESTION OF SABOTAGE by Bonnie J. Morris. 144 pp. A charming, sexy tale of romance, intrigue, and coming of age.
ISBN 0-9677753-8-8     $11.95

SLEIGHT OF HAND by Karin Kallmaker writing as Laura Adams. 256 pp. A journey of passion, heartbreak, and triumph that reunites two women for a final chance at their destiny.
ISBN 0-9677753-7-X     $11.95

MOVING TARGETS: A Helen Black Mystery by Pat Welch. 240 pp. Helen must decide if getting to the bottom of a mystery is worth hitting bottom.
ISBN 0-9677753-6-1     $11.95

CALM BEFORE THE STORM by Peggy J. Herring. 208 pp. Colonel Robicheaux retires from the military and comes out of the closet.
ISBN 0-9677753-1-0     $11.95

OFF SEASON by Jackie Calhoun. 208 pp. Pam threatens Jenny and Rita's fledgling relationship.
ISBN 0-9677753-0-2     $11.95

WHEN EVIL CHANGES FACE: A Motor City Thriller by Therese Szymanski. 240 pp. Brett Higgins is back in another heart-pounding thriller.
ISBN 0-9677753-3-7     $11.95

BOLD COAST LOVE by Diana Tremain Braund. 208 pp. Jackie Claymont fights for her reputation and the right to love the woman she chooses.
ISBN 0-9677753-2-9     $11.95

THE WILD ONE by Lyn Denison. 176 pp. Rachel never expected that Quinn's wild yearnings would change her life forever.
ISBN 0-9677753-4-5     $11.95

SWEET FIRE by Saxon Bennett. 224 pp. Welcome to Heroy—the town with the most lesbians per capita than any other place on the planet!
ISBN 0-9677753-5-3     $11.95